"We need to talk.

Wade conducted an about-face and bumped into Lindsay, who had followed him. He grabbed her arms to keep her from falling, his fingers sliding across her skin, the urge to draw her closer so powerful he shook with the effort to resist.

The green of her eyes drew him in, mesmerizing him. The curve of her full lower lip begged to be kissed. Wade swallowed hard on the rise of desire. He hadn't come to the Long K Ranch to rekindle a burned-out flame. His mission was to expose this woman's grandfather for attempted murder.

With all the self-control he could muster, his hands dropped to his sides, his fingers still tingling with her warmth. "Your grandfather said that if you want to talk to him, hurry up. He'd like to go to bed."

She pulled that full bottom lip between her teeth and chewed on it like she always had when she worked a problem in her head. "Okay. But we really need to talk."

"Tomorrow." Wade turned and left before he forgot why he'd come. Before he started thinking there might still be something between them, if he gave it a chance.

ELLE JAMES

COWBOY BRIGADE

TORONTO NEW YORK LONDON
AMSTERDAM PARIS SYDNEY HAMBURG
STOCKHOLM ATHENS TOKYO MILAN MADRID
PRAGUE WARSAW BUDAPEST AUCKLAND

Special thanks and acknowledgment to Elle James
for her contribution to the Daddy Corps series.

This book is dedicated to my husband
whose patience and understanding allows me to pursue my
dreams and follow my imagination in my writing career.
Love you, honey!

Recycling programs
for this product may
not exist in your area.

ISBN-13: 978-0-373-74602-6

COWBOY BRIGADE

Copyright © 2011 by Harlequin Books S.A.

ABOUT THE AUTHOR

Golden Heart Winner for Best Paranormal Romance in 2004, Elle James started writing when her sister issued a Y2K challenge to write a romance novel. She managed a full-time job, raised three wonderful children and she and her husband even tried their hands at ranching exotic birds (ostriches, emus and rheas) in the Texas Hill Country. Ask her, and she'll tell you what it's like to go toe to toe with an angry 350-pound bird! After leaving her successful career in information technology management, Elle is now pursuing her writing full-time. She loves building exciting stories about heroes, heroines, romance and passion. Elle loves to hear from fans. You can contact her at ellejames@earthlink.net or visit her website at www.ellejames.com.

Books by Elle James

HARLEQUIN INTRIGUE

CAST OF CHARACTERS

Wade Coltrane—Former Army Special Forces member whose specialty is infiltrating enemy lines, hired by Corps Security and Investigations to infiltrate the Long K Ranch.

Lindsay Kemp—Granddaughter of the owner of Long K Ranch who had the misfortune of falling in love with Wade Coltrane and now bears the secret of a night of passion between them.

Henry Kemp—Owner of the Long K Ranch who has a hatred of all things Lockhart and isn't afraid to tell everyone. Identified as a suspect who may be responsible for hiring a gunman to shoot Governor Lockhart, does his hatred of the Lockharts go deep enough to hire a killer?

Lila Lockhart—Governor of the state of Texas and potential candidate for the next U.S. presidential election. Her family is in jeopardy thanks to an unknown threat.

Bart Bellows—Wheelchair-bound owner of the Corps Security and Investigations Agency. Bart is an eccentric billionaire, a Vietnam vet and a former CIA agent determined to help others.

Frank Dorian—Recently hired ranch hand on the Long K Ranch who is aggressive, possessive and won't leave Lindsay Kemp alone.

Cal Murphy—Local pediatrician, Lindsay Kemp's ex-fiancé and Wade Coltrane's high school rival.

Prologue

"Hello, Bart." Governor Lila Lockhart spoke softly into the cell phone. With a bodyguard on either side, she had no privacy and it had been that way since the incident.

"Lila, I'm glad you called. Have there been any more threats?"

"Not since the Rory Stockett shooting, thank goodness. I just called to thank you and your team for all of your help. I couldn't have gotten through the past two weeks without knowing I had you watching my back."

"Lila, Rory was hired by someone and that someone still hasn't been found," Bart warned. "My men are still on full alert. I expect you to be equally vigilant."

"I am, believe me. I hate that all this is happening. I'm beginning to reconsider my options once this gubernatorial term is over."

"We'll find him, Lila. Don't go making rash decisions based on a crazy man taking potshots at you. You're not one to run. That's what I find most attractive about you."

Lila smiled. "Thanks, Bart. A little flattery always works wonders."

Bart chuckled. "My pleasure. Let me know if you need anything else. The men of Corps Security and Investigations are here to help see you through this."

Lila clicked the off button and leaned back in her seat, the smell of leather relaxing to her senses. It had been a grueling day of meetings, and she couldn't wait to get home and take a long hot bath.

It seemed a little odd thinking of getting naked in a bathtub with two very large, very strong bodyguards sitting on either side of her. A smile curved her lips. They would be appalled if they could read her mind.

Loud popping sounds erupted around her. The vehicle lurched and skidded sideways, metal screaming against pavement.

Lila clutched the armrest. "What's going on?"

The bodyguard on her left removed the Sig Sauer pistol from his shoulder holster and leaned forward, bracing his hand on the door.

The driver clung to the steering wheel, the veins standing out on his forehead as he fought to straighten the vehicle, but the wheels leaped over the shoulder of the road and the limo crashed downward into a ditch and up an embankment.

The bodyguard with the gun lost his grip on the weapon and grabbed for the armrest on the door.

With nothing to hold on to, Lila bounced in her seat, flung from side to side like a rag doll.

Barely able to view out the tinted windows, Lila didn't see the fencepost until the side of the car slammed into it. The bodyguard beside her crashed against the door, his head thumping the window. Bulletproof glass held true, even as the metal frame of the limo bent around the post. The bodyguard went limp.

Lila's seat belt held her in the middle, but the bodyguard on her other side hit her shoulder, jolting her hard, pain shooting through her neck and back.

When the world finally came to a jarring halt, the limo horn blared. Lila blinked and dragged in a deep breath, not having realized she'd been holding it since the first pop. The limo listed to the left, pointed back down the embankment at a forty-five degree angle. If not for the seat belt, Lila would have gone through the front windshield.

"Jimmy?" she called out to the driver.

His body slumped over the steering wheel, the source of the horn's blare.

"Jimmy!" Lila fiddled with the belt buckle.

"Governor Lockhart, please stay put." The bodyguard beside her reached out a hand too late to catch her.

The buckle opened and Lila fell across the open

space between the driver and where she and the bodyguards perched in the rear compartment, slamming headfirst into the back of the driver's seat.

Stunned, she pushed against the seat so that she could see Jimmy, her driver. Blood dripped down over his arm.

"Jimmy?" Lila felt for a pulse. For a moment she didn't feel one and her own heartbeat skittered to a halt. A second later, she could have cried out with joy. The faint thump of blood passing through a vein gave her hope that Jimmy would live.

"Help me out of here." She crawled up the side of the limo, pulling herself along by gripping the upholstery. "We have to get him help." She stared up at the bodyguard and across to his partner who hung like a crash dummy from the restraints. "What about Tom?"

"He's out, but his heartbeat is strong." The bodyguard above gave her a stern glare. "You have to stay inside the car while I check for trouble outside."

"I can't stand by and do nothing."

"Then find your cell phone and dial 9-1-1."

Her heart hammering against her ribs, Lila searched the tilted interior of the limo. It took her three precious minutes to locate her cell phone and even longer to reboot it to get it to work.

Her finger hit the speed dial for 9-1-1 and she relayed her location and the condition of the vehicle's occupants. Then she put the dispatcher on hold and speed dialed Bart.

"Lila?" Bart answered. "What's wrong?"

"It happened again."

Chapter One

Wade Coltrane stepped out of his truck and stared at the ranch house. Five years hadn't changed much. The paint was a little more worn, flaking off in a few places. The lawn could use cutting and the barn out behind the house had that weathered, old-wood look, but other than that, it appeared the same.

He tried to push back the feeling of having come home. He hadn't returned to the Long K Ranch to get comfortable and reminisce about old times, or to pick up where he'd left off. In many ways you could never go back. Time had a way of changing people, places and perspective.

Wade had come to secure employment with the ranch owner as cover for his real mission—spying on the one suspected of carrying out threats against Governor Lila Lockhart.

Second thoughts about his task had no place in his life. After the disaster of his military career, he needed this job and he needed to redeem himself. If not to anyone else, then in his own mind. He had a lot to atone for and nothing and nobody would get in the way of that atonement.

A pang of guilt sat like a wad of soggy sweat socks in his gut. Old Man Kemp had been his father's employer, the grumpy ranch owner had been tough but, for the most part, fair.

Wade had grown up on the ranch, playing in the barn, riding horses and swimming in the creek. Kemp's granddaughter had tagged along, getting in his way almost every step of the way.

Being the boss's kin, he'd put up with her.

An image of a redheaded hellion riding bareback at breakneck speeds across the pasture flashed across his memories.

Lindsay Kemp. Beautiful, passionate and fiercely independent and loyal. The boss's granddaughter. Completely out of his league, only he hadn't been bright enough to recognize it until too late.

A sigh rose up his chest and he swallowed hard. History had no place in the present other than as a reminder not to repeat one's mistakes.

Lindsay had forgotten him as soon as he left for boot camp. By the time he'd built his career in the Army and returned to ask her to marry him, she'd up and gotten herself engaged to a local doctor.

Just as well that she married a doctor. She'd have hated the life of a military spouse. And he hadn't been willing to give up his Army career. Then.

In five years, a lot could change.

Wade knocked at the door. When no one

answered, he rounded the house and headed for the barn. He spied movement in one of the training pens and altered his course.

A white-haired man, astride a sturdy bay gelding trotted around a well-worn circle inside the round pen. When he spied Wade, the old guy drew back on the reins, bringing the big gelding to a stop. Henry Kemp glared down at Wade with rheumy blue eyes. "We ain't buying anything."

"I'm not selling."

"You're trespassin'."

"I'm here to apply for the ranch hand job you posted at the Talk of the Town."

The old man's gaze traveled Wade's length. "Why should I hire you?"

"Because I know this ranch as well as you do, Mr. Kemp." Wade forced a grin he didn't feel. "Do you remember me, Mr. Kemp? Wade Coltrane. Jackson Coltrane's son."

"Little Wade Coltrane?" Henry slung his leg over the horse and eased to the ground. For a seventy-five-year-old man, Mr. Kemp got around pretty good.

Wade looked closer. The old guy got around but was it good enough to be a real threat to Governor Lockhart? This was the man suspected of hiring Rory Stockett to take a shot at her. The man who might have seeded the highway with horseshoe nails to cause the governor's limo to crash late last night?

Granted the old guy was a perpetual grump, a loudmouth and generally cantankerous, and he loved his granddaughter. A big plus in Wade's estimation.

But if Bart Bellows had good reason to believe Henry Kemp was threatening Governor Lockhart, who was Wade Coltrane, ex-soldier, to argue? He needed the job Bart offered, not only for the money, but also for a second chance.

Henry's eyes narrowed. "Why you hiding behind that beard?"

Wade rubbed the neatly trimmed facial hair. "Not hiding. The ladies tell me it's sexy."

The old man snorted. "That flyer must be three months old. I hired a ranch hand a long time ago. What do I need another one for?"

"I hear you've got some fences in need of repairing and roundup next week."

"And some people have big mouths. Where'd you learn all that?"

Wade reached out to stroke the soft muzzle of the gelding. "A couple of mutual acquaintances."

"I'd bet my Sunday shorts that was Stan and Fred. Those old coots ain't got a lick of sense."

"So…do you?"

Kemp's bushy white brows rose. "Do I what? Have a lick of sense? Hell, yeah."

Wade chuckled. "I know that, but do you have a need for a ranch hand who knows what he's doing and knows the lay of the land?"

"I tell you what I don't need, and that's a smart-mouth cowboy. Have you learned any better how to take orders?"

"Take 'em, and give 'em."

The old man glared down at him for a full minute before he spoke again. "You can have a rack in the bunkhouse. Dinner's at the big house at six-thirty sharp. If you're not there, you don't eat."

With a tip of his hat, Wade stood with his foot on the lower fence rail. "Thanks, Mr. Kemp."

"Don't thank me. And don't make me regret hiring you."

The old man had walked right into Wade's trap, believing his story hook, line and sinker. The first step in his infiltration was successful, Wade walked away, his sights set on mission accomplishment. Nothing would get in his way.

LINDSAY KEMP STEERED the rickety ranch truck through the arching gateway of the Long K Ranch. Lyric and Lacey leaned against each other in the backseat of the crew cab, buckled into their booster seats, sound asleep. They usually fell asleep on the way home from the Cradles to Crayons Daycare where they spent two days of the week in the mother's day-out program. Lindsay couldn't really afford it, but the girls needed time to play with children their own age. And Lindsay needed the break to handle things in town and on the ranch without four-year-old, identical twins underfoot.

She glanced in the rearview mirror at the black-haired girls and marveled at how they didn't look a bit like her. Neither child had auburn hair, gray-green eyes or even a single freckle like their mother.

Their biological father had strong genes. He'd been the spitting image of his father, thick black hair, blue eyes and high cheekbones. Somewhere in their ancestry was Apache Indian blood, thus the hair and cheekbones.

Too bad the girls would never know their father and their father would never know them. Because he'd dedicated himself to a career in the Army, Lindsay hadn't wanted to place a burden on him by telling him that she was pregnant. Almost five years later, the opportunity to enlighten him was well past.

Lindsay glanced at her watch. Crap!

She had exactly ten minutes to get the girls into the house, get herself changed and catch the horses before Zachary showed up for his riding lesson. Stacy, Zachary's mother, always arrived five minutes early.

Lindsay pressed her foot to the accelerator, roaring down the gravel road toward the ranch house. She skidded to a stop in front of the only home she'd ever known, slammed the truck into Park and jumped out.

"Girls, let's get you inside. Come on. Wake up."

Lacey perked up and stared around, her eyes

blinking. "Can I have a grilled cheese sandwich?" Lindsay lifted her out of the truck and set her on her feet

"Maybe after riding lessons, unless Grandpa can make it for you."

Lacey trudged toward the house, her forehead wrinkled in a frown. "He burns them. I want you to make me one."

"Then it'll have to wait until after lessons."

Lyric remained fast asleep on the backseat, having tipped over.

Her pale skin and bright pink lips looked angelic. Lindsay didn't have the heart to wake her. Despite her aching back, she lifted the child and carried her into the house where she laid her on the couch in the living room.

"Gramps," Lindsay shouted, hurrying down the hallway to her room.

"That you, Lindsay?" a coarse voice called from the study.

"Yes, sir. I'm late for my riding lessons. Can I bother you to keep an eye on the girls?"

"Bother?" Her grandfather appeared in the doorway to his office. "Since when are my great-granddaughters a bother?"

"You're a dream, Gramps." Lindsay ducked into her room and yanked a well-worn chambray shirt and equally worn jeans from her closet. "Lacey wants a grilled cheese sandwich. She can wait until I get done with lessons."

"I'm old, not dead. I can manage a little girl's sandwich," her grandfather groused.

Lindsay had learned long ago that Grandpa Kemp's bark was much worse than his bite. Even the twins had him figured out. Too bad not everyone in Freedom, Texas, understood Henry Kemp. He griped fiercely, and he loved fiercely.

"Gramps, she doesn't like it burned. Give her a drink and an apple. I'll make the sandwich when I'm done."

"I'm perfectly capable of making a sandwich," he grumbled. "But have it your way."

"Thanks, Gramps." Lindsay smiled inside her room, slipping out of her nicest jeans and into worn denim. After lessons, she'd be mucking stalls. No use damaging her only good pair of jeans. "They can come out when they're fully awake and have had their snack." Lindsay stripped her best white blouse off and shoved her arms into the chambray shirt.

"Yes, ma'am. Am I getting that old that I'm taking orders from my granddaughter now?"

Lindsay buttoned as she hurried down the hall. She stopped to briefly kiss her grandfather's cheek. "You're always the boss, Gramps. I love you."

The old man rubbed a hand to the place she'd kissed, a frown clearing from his forehead. "Damn, right."

"Watch your language." Lindsay sprinted through

the house, grabbing sugar cubes from the jar on the table beside the back door.

"I hired a new ranch hand today," her grandfather called out behind her.

Lindsay stumbled. What? She didn't have time to stop and go back to question him. A new ranch hand? They couldn't afford to pay the hands they had. The weight of the world bore down on her shoulders. How could she get it through her grandfather's head that they didn't have any money?

She'd just have to apologize to the new hand and send him packing before he put in too many hours. Easy enough. Dealing with her grandfather was an entirely different challenge.

For now she needed to focus on the only lucrative business on the place. The riding lessons, which had started as a way to make a little extra income for her and the girls, had grown into a financial supplement for the ranch. Until they brought in the herd and sent them off to auction, they were pretty well broke. The riding school put food on the table for Lindsay's family and the ranch hands until cash flow improved.

An SUV pulled to a halt in front of the barn. Stacy Giordano climbed down and waved at Lindsay. "Hey, girl, sorry I'm late. It's been insane at the governor's place."

"Hi, Stacy." Lindsay hurried toward Stacy. "I'm running late, too."

"Did you hear about the governor's accident last night?"

Lindsay ground to a halt in front of the vehicle, her stomach flip-flopping. "Accident?"

"Yeah, I spent my day at the hospital with the governor, her bodyguards and her driver."

"Holy smokes. What happened?"

"Not sure yet, but they think someone threw nails all over the road. Two of the tires blew and sent them into a ditch."

"Is everyone all right?"

Stacy nodded. "Mostly minor injuries, but the driver suffered a concussion."

"Any idea who might have done it?"

"Not yet. The sheriff is checking into it. In the meantime, we've had to tighten security even more. Much tighter and we won't be able to breathe."

"I'm sorry to hear that."

Stacy opened the back door to her SUV and helped her son down.

"Hey, Zachary, good to see you." Lindsay turned toward the barn. "You guys wait just a minute while I catch Whiskers."

"I can wait, but Zachary will be chomping at the bit to ride."

Lindsay smiled and waved at Zachary as she passed by. "Let him stand by the fence while I get a bridle." She stopped again, dug in her pocket and turned to the boy. "Here, you can help me. Hold out your hand with this and Whiskers will come to you." She pressed a sugar cube into the boy's hand and curled his fingers around it.

Zachary stared at his closed hand.

"Come on, Zachary. Let's go see if Whiskers will come to you." Stacy took his other hand and led him toward the wood-rail fence.

Lindsay raced into the barn grabbing a bridle from the nail on the wall.

A movement in the shadows made her jump.

Frank Dorian pushed away from the wall he'd been leaning on, a pitchfork in his hand, the stall beside him open and untouched.

"Are you supposed to be cleaning the stalls?" she asked.

Frank shrugged. "Maybe."

Anger flared and Lindsay came to a complete halt in front of the big cowboy her grandfather had hired several weeks ago. He had issues taking orders from a woman.

Lindsay didn't have issues with calling him on it. "Either you are or you aren't. Which is it?"

The man stepped up to her and looked down his nose into her eyes. "I can think of a lot more interesting things to do in a barn than mucking stalls." He reached out and trailed his finger down her arm.

Lindsay knocked his hand away, rage burning a path up her chest into her cheeks. "Don't. Ever. Touch me again." She glared at him, her lips pressed tightly together. "Do you understand?"

He stepped closer, his chest pushing against hers. "Or what?"

Her heart hammering behind her rib cage, Lindsay refused to step back, refused to back down. "Or I'll have your butt fired so fast you won't know what happened."

"Your grandfather hired me."

"And I'm telling you, I can fire you." She narrowed her eyes at him. "Care to test the theory?"

Frank leaned down, his lips next to her ear. "Just so you know, no one fires Frank Dorian."

A shadow blocked the sun streaming in through the barn's open double doors. "Is there a problem here?"

The low, resonant voice raised gooseflesh along Lindsay's arms. If she wasn't so distracted by Frank, she'd swear the voice was familiar. Only one man she'd ever known had the ability to make her shiver all over. "Is there a problem, Frank?" Lindsay asked the man who'd just threatened her.

"No problem." Frank stepped away from Lindsay and entered the dirty stall, pitchfork in hand.

As soon as he moved, a broad-chested man came into view. With his back to the outside door, his face remained in the shadows.

"Can I help you?" Lindsay asked, moving closer, the hairs on the back of her neck standing at attention, her knees suddenly wobbly.

"I thought maybe I could help you."

That voice again.

Lindsay clutched the bridle with nerveless fingers, all the blood draining from her face. It couldn't be. Not now. Not him.

As though dragged by an invisible rope, she moved closer until she could see the man's face.

She gasped, her hand going to her throat and then reaching out toward him. He had to be a mirage. "Wade?"

The man with ice-blue eyes and coal-black hair nodded. "Hello, Ms. Kemp. Or should I say Mrs. Murphy?"

Chapter Two

Wade stared down into Lindsay's gray-green eyes, drinking in every detail of her face from the finely arched brows to her stubborn chin and the freckles sprinkled liberally across the bridge of her nose and cheeks. She'd pulled her glorious mane of fiery auburn hair up into a loose, messy knot, but curling wisps had escaped, framing her face, giving her a vulnerable appearance, belying her strength and fierce independence.

She took his breath away.

"What…" She gulped and started again. "What are you doing here? I thought you were in Iraq, Afghanistan or somewhere dangerous."

He shook his head. "Not anymore, unless you consider the Long K Ranch dangerous." He had been in both Iraq and Afghanistan, and to hell and back. Nothing could be as bad as being in the sandbox of the Middle East.

"Why here?" Lindsay whispered. "Why now?"

"I'm home. Your grandfather hired me on as a ranch hand."

Lindsay's face paled and she blinked several times, her body swaying.

Wade reached for her, afraid she'd fall.

"No!" She held up her hand, knocking his away. "I don't need you."

"Sorry. You looked like you were going to faint."

She squared her shoulders and looked down her nose at him. "Kemps don't faint." Even though she tried hard to look strong, her words shook, belying her tough stance.

As stubborn and beautiful as ever.

Seeing her made his chest ache. Wade forced himself to look away. "What are you doing here?" he asked.

"I have a riding lesson to teach. Not that it's any of your business."

"Don't you have better things to do in town?"

"I can't imagine anything better than teaching disabled children to ride, can you?"

He smiled and brushed a hand along her cheek. As soon as he felt the smoothness of her skin, he regretted reaching out to her. But he couldn't help himself. "Always taking care of people, aren't you?"

"Yes. You got a problem with that?" She knocked his hand away again. "I take my work seriously."

He'd expected her to be a full-time assistant for her husband, the good Dr. Murphy. He'd counted on it and could kick himself for his automatic response to her nearness, his desire to hold her, touch her, feel her lips against his.

Lindsay Kemp's face had been what kept him alive throughout his captivity, what gave him the will to take the next breath. Even though he knew she'd married, that they could never be together, he'd lived to see her face again. "I would have thought you'd be working with the doctor now."

Her auburn brows wrinkled. "Why would you think that?

"I didn't think you'd still be working out here." And if she worked at the Long K Ranch on a regular basis, his mission would be in jeopardy—his focus compromised. "What does your husband think of you coming out here?"

Her brows sank deeper over her eyes. "Husband?" Then her eyes widened and she shook her head. "I'm not married to Cal Murphy, if that's what you're thinking."

Wade stepped back, his heart skipping several beats before it slammed into his rib cage at a million beats per minute. "Not married? But I thought…"

"If you'd bothered to keep in touch, you'd have known that. Now, if you'll excuse me…" She pushed around him, hurrying toward the saddle racks where she selected a child's saddle and flung it over her shoulder.

As if he'd just been punched in the gut, Wade stood rooted to the barn floor struggling to remem-

ber how to breathe. "What happened? Last time I
was here, you were engaged."

"It didn't happen." She marched toward the barn
door, her gaze fully averted from him, she refused
to meet his eyes.

Stunned by her revelation, it took Wade several
seconds to come to grips. He sprang forward, blocking her exit. "Why?"

She stared up into his eyes. "Not because of you,
if that's what you think."

He let the breath out that he'd been holding,
slowly so that she couldn't tell how much her answer
had meant to him, and how much it hurt. "Let me
help you." He reached for the saddle, lifting it
effortlessly.

"I don't need help." She jerked away, her face
flaming a dull red. "I've managed on my own for
years."

"I know you don't need help, but I work here now.
Let me do my job."

"As for that…we'll see." She clutched the bridle to
her chest with one hand and yanked the saddle from
his hands with the other. "In the meantime, don't
bother to unpack. I want to talk to my grandfather
first."

Lindsay marched out of the barn, her head held
high like a queen.

With every ounce of his strength he fought to keep
from following her, dragging her into his arms and

kissing her so thoroughly that she'd forget all about Cal Murphy and the five years he'd been away.

Snickering from the stall behind him made Wade come to his senses faster than his own ability to talk himself down. Until that moment, he'd completely forgotten the man named Frank was still in the same barn with him.

Frank stood leaning on his pitchfork a smirk curling one side of his mouth. "She isn't any more interested in you than she is me."

"Shut up, Frank." Wade stalked to the pile of feed sacks stacked inside the barn door and slung one over his shoulder. Flinging a fifty-pound bag of feed did nothing toward slowing his heart rate or reining in the rampant thoughts racing through his head. And Frank's smirking attitude just made him want to hit someone.

Lindsay wasn't married to Cal Murphy.

Wade ripped open the bag and poured sweet feed into one of the feed bins. Back at the stack of feed bags, he hefted another onto his shoulder.

Why hadn't she married Cal? Was she still living at the Long K Ranch?

One question after another rolled over in his mind until they began repeating themselves.

He'd come to Freedom, Texas, fully expecting to find Lindsay Kemp married and gone from the ranch. If he'd known she was still here, he never would have agreed to go undercover to expose her grandfather.

At that moment he couldn't get past the one truth.

Lindsay Kemp wasn't married.

He dumped the last bag of feed into the bin and straightened.

Frank stood looking at him, still leaning on the pitchfork.

Wade glared at Frank. "Gets done quicker if you actually work at it."

"What do you care? She'll have you out of here so fast you won't know what hit you."

Not if I can help it. With his jaw set, his fingers clenched, Wade strode out of the barn and directly to the big house. He had to talk to Henry Kemp before Lindsay got back to him.

FIVE-YEAR-OLD Zachary ran around in circles, stopping every two or three spins to gather rocks from the ground and line them up in a neat row. He still held the sugar cube clenched in his fist.

Lindsay smiled. Stacy had her hands full with Zachary. Twins were difficult at times, but an energetic autistic child had to be even harder to cope with.

"Zachary, why don't you feed Whiskers his sugar cube?" Lindsay suggested.

The boy immediately stopped running and held out his hand with the damp lump of sugar.

Whiskers plucked it from his palm with his big, velvety lips.

Zachary giggled and pulled his hand back, wiping it against the side of his jeans.

Lindsay tossed a blanket on the horse and settled the saddle in place over it.

"Who's the hunk with the beard?" Stacy asked.

Without looking at her friend, Lindsay reached beneath the horse for the leather strap. "Does it matter?"

"Not that I'm in the market or anything, but he's definitely drool-worthy. Spill, girl, who is he?"

"Wade Coltrane." Lindsay shoved the leather strap through the girth ring and pulled up on it a little harder than necessary.

Whiskers puffed out his belly and danced a few steps away from her.

"Sorry, boy." Lindsay smoothed a hand down the horse's nose.

Stacy tipped her head to the side. "Wade Coltrane…" Her eyes widened and a grin spread across her face. "*The* Wade Coltrane you used to talk about? Weren't you two a thing back in high school?"

"That was ages ago. People change. Some grow up and move on." Lindsay didn't like the way this conversation was going. "I'm glad you've been bringing Zachary here. He seems to like the horses."

"He loves it. If nothing else, he's getting fresh air and sunshine." Stacy planted her hands on her hips. "You're changing the subject."

"Yeah, the other subject is off-limits."

"Off-limits?" Stacy pouted. "You're no fun. Just when we were getting somewhere with Wade."

"I'm not getting anywhere with him. Apparently my grandfather hired him. I can just as easily fire him." She straightened and glanced down at Zachary. "Ready to ride?"

Zachary danced in place, staring up at the horse, his eyes rounded.

"Let me get him up there. I never know how he'll react." Stacy pulled her son into her arms, talking to him in soothing tones. "Hey, sweetie, Whiskers wants to take you for a ride."

Lindsay steadied the horse, stroking the big animal's back as Stacy settled Zachary in the saddle.

As though a switch had been turned, Zachary calmed and sat still, a smile spreading across his little face.

Lindsay loved this part of her job. When a disabled child made a connection with the animal, all her efforts seemed worth it. It didn't pay much, but every little bit helped and the rewards were far deeper than monetary.

She adjusted the stirrups to fit the length of the boy's legs, and handed him the reins, laying them in his hands the way a western rider should hold them. With her fingers hooked through the bridle close to the horse's mouth, Lindsay looked up at the boy. "Ready, Zachary?"

The child grunted and rocked in his saddle. He was ready.

As Lindsay walked the horse around the ring, her thoughts strayed to the man she'd left in the barn.

Her stomach did a complete flip-flop. Wade Coltrane had returned to Freedom. Oh God, why now? She'd spent the last five years trying her hardest to forget the man. He'd blown through on leave five years ago, just when she thought she'd gotten over him the first time, upended her life and left.

Lindsay had agreed to marry Cal Murphy, the most eligible bachelor in town. All her financial woes would have been solved and she would have been married to a rock-solid, honest-to-goodness nice guy.

Then Wade showed up, wearing his Class A greens, his hair cut high and tight, clean-shaven and so handsome that he took her breath away. He'd rocked her world all over again.

She'd thrown everything out the window when he'd taken her in his arms and made mad, passionate love to her. She'd forgotten her promise to Cal, forgotten the years she'd pined for Wade, forgotten everything…including birth control.

When she'd woken up in his truck the next morning, she'd been so horrified that she'd betrayed Cal, she'd told Wade to leave.

And he had. He left and shortly after returning to his duty station, Wade was deployed to Iraq.

Two weeks later, Lindsay discovered she was pregnant.

When she'd broken the news to Cal, he'd demanded a DNA test. Cal wasn't the father.

Lindsay knew it had to be Wade. When the girls were born with thick black hair and blue eyes, all doubt disappeared.

The sound of girls giggling reached her ears, bringing her out of the past and back to the present.

"Oh God, the girls!" She nearly dropped the reins and ran from the pen.

One look at Zachary reminded her that she couldn't end the lesson now. The little boy needed the structure of set times and routines to make him comfortable. Lindsay couldn't do anything but what she got paid to do.

She looked up toward the house and nearly had a heart attack.

Wade walked toward her, Lyric and Lacey skipping along beside him, each holding one of his big hands. He looked so natural, like he belonged with the girls. And they looked just like their father.

Five years of guilt rose in her throat like bile.

She hadn't known how to tell him then. He'd been deployed, she'd sent him away. It was easier to go on with life on her own, carrying the big secret with her. No one knew except Lindsay who the twins' father was.

Seeing them together, how could anyone miss the resemblance?

"Tall, dark, handsome and with the added bonus

of being good with children." Stacy grinned at Lindsay. "If you're not calling dibs, can I?"

"No!" Lindsay said the one word with such force that Whiskers jerked against the bit, jarring Zachary.

The boy dropped the reins and gripped the saddle horn, his face crinkling in a frown.

"Sorry about that, Zachary." Lindsay stroked the boy's leg, gathered the reins and handed them to him again. She and Zachary both needed calming after her outburst. One more reason she couldn't have Wade Coltrane working at the Long K Ranch. She wouldn't get any work done knowing he was around. Not that she cared for him. She was long over her girlish infatuation.

The twins had readjusted her focus on what was more important. Providing them a good home was the number one goal in Lindsay's mind.

Lyric and Lacey smiled and laughed all the way to the fence where Stacy stood.

"Look what I found. More students for riding lessons." He grinned at Lindsay, his gaze challenging her.

What could she say in front of the girls? Afraid she'd blurt out the truth, Lindsay kept her lips tightly shut.

Wade swung Lacey up in his arms and perched her on the rail in front of him.

"Me! Do me!" Lyric raised her hands.

Wade swung her up to sit beside her sister, a hand

on each girl to keep them from falling into the pen. "How many children do you teach?" Wade asked.

"A few." Lindsay guarded her words, her gaze shooting from the girls to Wade and across to Stacy whose eyes had narrowed. She raised a finger and tapped her lips.

Please don't say anything, Lindsay begged silently. She didn't want Stacy to state the obvious.

Based on his easy rapport with the twins, Wade hadn't put the pieces together. He didn't see himself in the miniature versions of him right under his nose.

If she didn't have an autistic child riding a horse that she was leading, Lindsay might have given in to the urge to run screaming from the pen.

"I want to ride next," Lacey demanded.

"I want to ride next," Lyric parroted.

Wade laughed and turned to Stacy. "Hi, I'm Wade Coltrane, the new ranch hand." He held out his hand.

Stacy took it, a grin spreading across her pretty face.

At that moment, Lindsay could have scratched her friend's eyes right out of her head.

She wanted to scream *Hands off!*

But she couldn't. Five years ago, she'd made it clear that she didn't want Wade in her life. Now that she had the girls, she had them to consider. And she didn't want Wade back if the only reason was the girls.

Lindsay closed her eyes and counted to five. What the heck was she thinking? The girls were as much his as they were hers. He was bound to figure it out sooner or later. Better to tell him, let him get all mad and hope it blows over so she can get on with her life as a single mother.

But not now. Not here. And not in front of the girls and Stacy.

And did she really think he'd let it blow over? Let her continue on with full custody of their girls like their father never existed?

Her feet dragged in the dust of the pen as she led Whiskers in a circle.

The steady, ordered life she'd carefully constructed for the girls was about to change and she could do very little to stop it.

"Mommy, can I ride Little Joe?" Lacey called out.

"Mommy, can I ride Sweetie Pie?" Lyric asked.

Lindsay stared across the length of the pen, her gaze capturing Wade's as realization dawned on him.

That look of utter shock could not be faked. He stared at her and then down at the girls. "These girls are yours?"

Chapter Three

A hundred questions barreled through Wade's head. Lindsay had twin daughters? Who was the father? Where was he now? Did he live at the ranch with Lindsay? Where did Cal Murphy fit in the picture? Was Cal the father?

Wade stared at the tops of the girls' heads. Lindsay had children.

Anger followed closely behind the shock. If Cal was the father, why the hell didn't he step up to the responsibility of raising his own children? Why hadn't he married Lindsay?

"Zachary, sweetie, the lesson is over for now." Lindsay stopped the horse at the rail in front of Stacy and gave her a weak smile. "I'm sorry, Stacy, I just can't do it today." She reached up and hooked Zachary beneath the arms.

He clung to the saddle horn and grunted, his face wrinkling in a fierce frown. "Ride!"

Wade placed the girls on the ground and entered the pen with Lindsay. "Hey, big guy, let me help you down."

The little boy's eyes rounded and his gaze darted from Lindsay to Stacy and back to Wade.

When Wade reached up for him, Zachary let go of the horn and let Wade lift him off. As soon as he cleared the saddle, he reached for his mother.

Stacy took him in her arms and hugged him. "It's okay, Zachary. Mr. Coltrane is a nice man. He just wants to help." She looked across at Lindsay, her brows rising as if in silent question.

Lindsay shook her head. "I'll see you the day after tomorrow at the fundraiser, right?"

"Right. I kinda have to be there." Stacy laughed. "Seeing as I'm organizing it. And if you're in town before then, call me, we can do lunch." She held her thumb and pinky to her face like she was talking into a telephone and mouthed the words *call me*.

"Yeah, I will," Lindsay lied. She loved Stacy, but the last thing she wanted to do was talk to her best friend about Wade Coltrane. Not yet, not when she didn't know what to do or say. She led Whiskers out of the pen and toward the barn.

"Can I ride Whiskers now?" Lacey danced beside Lindsay out of range of the horse's hooves.

"Not now. I have to get supper on the table. Maybe tomorrow morning when it's nice and cool outside."

Lacey's face puckered in a frown. "But I want to ride now."

"I want to ride, too." Lyric caught up with Lacey and automatically reached for her sister's hand.

"You can help me brush Whiskers. How about that?"

Both girls hopped up and down. "Yay! We get to brush Whiskers!"

Lindsay thanked God for the buffer her girls created, delaying the inevitable confrontation with Wade. "As long as you're working here, and I'm not saying that it will last, you can bring in the horses from the pasture. They need to be fed."

Wade's eyes narrowed as if he could read her mind and knew she was stalling. "We need to talk."

No, we don't. She led Whiskers into the barn and tied him to the outside of his stall, completely ignoring the man she'd left standing in the barnyard. Out of the corner of her eye she could see him watching her and her skin twitched, her heart beating ninety-to-nothing, the mind-numbing, breath-stealing sexual attraction she'd always felt toward Wade still palpable and real. When he turned and walked toward the pasture to bring in the horses, she breathed a sigh and vowed to make quick work of brushing Whiskers so that she could get to the house before Wade.

She had to talk with her grandfather. Wade Coltrane couldn't work at the Long K Ranch. After he discovered the girls were his, he'd be impossible to avoid. At least if he lived in town, they'd only meet when he had his scheduled visitation.

Lindsay grabbed two hard-bristled brushes and a

curry comb, handing the brushes to the girls. "Stand on either side of his head so that he can see you. I don't want him to spook and kick you."

Lacey ducked beneath Whiskers's chin and brushed as high as she could reach. Lyric spent her time petting the horse's soft nose, the brush forgotten in her other hand.

Meanwhile, Lindsay removed the saddle and blanket, storing them on the saddle rack before hurrying to the feed bin where she scooped up a bucket of sweet feed. She was hooking the bucket to the inside of Whiskers's stall when Wade led two horses into the barn.

"Where do you want them?" he asked.

"The sorrel mare is Sweetie Pie, she goes in the end stall. Little Joe is the bay, he goes next to Sweetie Pie." Lindsay turned to the girls. "Okay, I'll finish up. You two go on up to the house and wash your hands. You can help me cook dinner."

"Can we have macaroni and cheese?" Lacey asked, her blue eyes sparkling so much like Wade's in the light shining in through the open barn door.

"I thought you wanted grilled cheese sandwiches."

Lacey bounced up and down. "We want macaroni and cheese now."

"Yeah, macaroni and cheese." Lyric took her sister's hand, grinning.

"Okay." How could Lindsay refuse when they

looked so eager? "But you have to eat your green beans, too."

Both girls shouted, "Yay!" Then they handed their brushes to Lindsay and ran for the door.

Lindsay realized her mistake as she stood with the brushes in her hand, alone in the barn with Wade. She grabbed Whiskers's bridle and led him into the stall, closing the gate behind her. Taking her time, she finished currying the horse, while she held her breath, willing Wade to go back out to the pasture. As soon as he left, she could escape to the house and have that conversation with her grandfather.

She must have groomed the horse twice before she realized she had stalled long enough. Lindsay slipped the bridle from Whiskers's head and ducked out the stall door. The barn was empty. Wade had left. Sweetie Pie nickered from her stall, wanting her feed.

"Can't you wait until Wade feeds you?" Lindsay called out softly.

Sweetie Pie nickered again and Little Joe added his protest, stomping his foot in the hard-packed dirt.

"Really? You can't wait? But I can't stick around. I can't do this now. I'm not ready." Her heart banging against her ribs, her body tense with the urge to flee, Lindsay looked from the horses to the open barn door. She sighed, grabbed two buckets and scooped up sweet feed—one for Sweetie Pie and one for Little Joe—and hung them inside their stall doors.

Still no sign of Wade or the other horses he was supposed to bring in. "You got lucky this time," she muttered to herself, heading for the barn door. "He's going to corner you sooner or later and will want to know the truth."

"Truth about what?" Wade rounded the corner of the barn door, leading a dappled gray gelding and a golden palomino mare.

Lindsay's face burned. "I wasn't talking to you."

Wade smiled, his blue eyes twinkling just like Lacey's had only minutes before.

Lindsay's chest tightened. That smile had gotten her into more trouble than she could have ever imagined five years ago. It still had the effect of turning her knees to rubber.

Granted, he looked different. No longer the clean-cut soldier who'd come home on leave. He sported a dark, neatly trimmed beard that made him look even more dangerous and…sexier than ever.

"I always liked it that you talked to your horses." He didn't move, he and the horses more or less blocking Lindsay's escape route.

"I understand them and I like to think they understand me." She shrugged, wishing she had made her run for the house when she'd had the chance. This conversation reminded her of others equally as intimate in the setting and content.

Anxious to leave him, but not wanting him to know just how he affected her, Lindsay strode forward and reached for the dappled gray gelding. "Come on, Stormy. You'll be wanting your feed." When her hand touched Wade's, that same old shocking electric current coursed through her veins, headed directly south. Heat flared throughout her body, igniting a flame she'd thought burned out five years ago.

She jerked the reins from Wade's hand and practically ran for Stormy's stall. Why did she have to be so aware of this man? He'd broken her heart more than once, hadn't she learned her lesson?

After she got Stormy into his stall, she shoved the latch closed and turned to run for the house.

Before she could take two steps, Wade had the mare's stall door closed and he'd spun to face her.

Lindsay sidestepped him, but he didn't let her pass, grabbing her by the arms.

"Look, Lindsay, I'm not here to start something between you and me. I know that's over. I'm just here because I need a job."

Where his fingers curled around her arms her skin tingled, reminding Lindsay of the last time he'd held her. The magic of their lovemaking and how much she had wanted to be with him always. The depth of all that emotion pressed against her chest, making it impossible for her to breathe, much less talk.

Her eyes blurred and she realized in horror that

she would cry if she didn't get away from him. And no matter what she did, she refused to cry in front of Wade Coltrane. She'd done enough crying over this man and, as her grandfather would lecture, Kemps don't cry.

Forcing air past her vocal cords, she said, "I don't want you here, no matter what your reasons."

For a brief moment, a sadness so deep it almost hurt her to see flashed in his blue eyes. Then it was gone and his hands fell to his sides, his lips firming into a straight line. "I understand. And I hope you'll understand that I work for your grandfather." He spun on his heels and walked out of the barn.

Lindsay stared at his back, anger replacing sadness and the lingering waves of lust of a moment ago. "How dare he talk to me that way?" She pushed her sleeves up and stomped toward the house. Her grandfather would see it her way and fire Wade Coltrane's butt quicker than he could say *I'm sorry.*

When she reached the house, the girls waited in the kitchen clean and ready to start cooking supper. Her grandfather was nowhere to be found.

Damn.

WADE FED the horses and turned them back out to pasture before he grabbed his worn, military duffle bag from the truck and headed for the bunkhouse to clean up. Frank beat him there, his booted feet propped on the footboard of his bunk.

"Surprise, surprise," Wade muttered to himself. Out loud he asked, "Where are the other hands?"

"Out with Old Man Kemp, shoring up the cattle chutes, gettin' them ready for roundup. Why do you care?"

"I care because I work here and, if they need help, I should be out there."

"They'll be back any minute for supper. Lindsay sure can rustle up some fine grub. Not only is she good-lookin', she's a good cook. Everything a man could want in a woman." Frank stuck a hay straw in his mouth, his gaze narrowed as if waiting for a rise from Wade.

Wade tamped down the anger quick to rise when Frank made mention of Lindsay in any way. He ignored the guy and stared around the bunkhouse. "Which bunks aren't taken?"

"Those." Frank jerked his head past his bunk to the ones where thin mattresses lay bare on the bed frames.

Dorian's gaze followed him as Wade moved past. "Hear you used to live on the ranch."

Wade found a wooden footlocker beside the bed, opened it and shoved his duffle bag into it without unpacking. "You heard right." He unbuckled the lock on the bag, grabbed out a shaving kit, towel and clean clothes.

"Prior Army?" Dorian asked.

"Yup. What about you?"

"Same. Did some time on active duty." Frank

crossed his arms behind his head. "Why come back to this podunk town?"

"Needed a job." Wade gathered his things and straightened.

Wade could care less about Frank and his past but, as a new hired hand, he had to try to fit in, even if he didn't plan to stay long. As soon as he had the evidence he needed, he'd be gone from the Long K Ranch. "What's your story?"

Frank shrugged. "Same."

The bunkhouse door opened and two men walked in shaking dust from their cowboy hats.

The first guy, a short, grizzled older man, with a scraggly white beard and skin as tough as leather, tossed his cowboy hat onto the first bed. He held out his hand to Wade. "Roy Kingery, folks call me Dusty."

Wade smiled, shook hands with Dusty and introduced himself.

The second man, tall, thin as a rail and with facial features as gaunt as Abraham Lincoln, strode in, head down, still wearing his cowboy hat. He didn't say anything, walked straight to his bed and unlaced well-worn leather chaps.

Dusty jerked his head toward the tall lean man. "That's Billy Moore. He don't talk much, but ain't a man who can out-rope, outride or outshoot him in the county."

Wade nodded toward Billy. "Good to know you."

He glanced pointedly at the items in his hands. "Dinner's at six-thirty, right?"

"Yup, and you don't want to be late for Miss Lindsay's cookin'. She might ride as good as the rest of us, but she also knows her way around the kitchen."

"Guess I better get cleaned up." Wade strode the length of the bunkhouse aware of the men's gazes following him, summing him up.

The bunkhouse reminded Wade of old World War II barracks with a neat row of bunks on each side and a communal latrine and shower facility at one end. If he hadn't been through all that he had, he'd almost feel like a new recruit at boot camp.

He wasn't the green trainee he had been all those years ago. The months he'd spent fighting in Afghanistan and Iraq had sharpened his fighting skills, but the time he'd been held captive in a Taliban terrorist camp had marked him for life.

His fingers rose to the scar near his right eye, memories flooding in to remind him of what he'd been subjected to. The body had a way of forgetting pain, but he could never forget what he'd done. Neither could he forgive himself for cracking.

He showered quickly, toweling off as the other men wandered in naked, bars of soap in hand.

Wade hurried through shaving, dressed in jeans and a clean black T-shirt, and pulled his boots on. He wanted a chance to speak with Old Man Kemp before supper. If Lindsay had already gotten to him, his mission could be over before it even started. No matter what Lindsay said, Wade would keep this job if he had to trick Old Man Kemp into agreeing to it.

With the three ranch hands still washing up, Wade climbed the slight rise to the ranch house. As he passed by an open window, Lindsay's voice carried to him on the warm, late-summer breeze.

"We don't need another ranch hand, Gramps. We can't afford the ones we have."

Wade stopped outside the window to Henry Kemp's office and stood beside a tree, out of view, tamping down the surge of guilt he felt for eavesdropping on a man who'd done him a favor by hiring him.

Yet Old Man Kemp was his target. He had to eavesdrop to know what he had planned. If the man really did want to harm Governor Lockhart, Wade had to find the evidence that would put him away before he succeeded

"Roundup is next week," Henry said. "Surely we can afford to keep him at least one week. Besides, I liked the Coltranes. It was a sad day when his old man died in that flash flood. Wade's daddy did good work for us. It's the least I can do for an old friend."

Wade remembered that day when Henry Kemp came to the high school. Wade had been a senior then, staring out the window at the rain clouds. The guys had been excited that football practice would be wet that day. Coach never skipped practice. They'd be playing in the mud and, just like when they were all kids, they loved playing in the mud.

Henry had taken him out of that classroom that day to tell him that his father had died at a low-water crossing. He and his horse had been swept downstream. The horse made it, but Jackson Coltrane didn't.

His chest tight, Wade forced himself to listen to the conversation.

"Gramps, what will we pay him with? The bank account is down to nothing. We haven't been paid for the last ten steers we sold at auction, and I'm not having any luck getting a bank to loan us money to tide us over until roundup. We're broke."

Wade leaned out enough to catch a glimpse of Lindsay's face. With color high in her cheeks and her green eyes flashing, she'd never been more beautiful.

Henry slammed his palm flat on the desk. "Damn Lockharts!"

"Oh, please." Lindsay flung her hand in the air and spun away from her grandfather. "Why bring them up? What happened with them was years ago."

"Yeah, but they tricked me into selling that land to them. While they're sitting all fat, rich and happy, we're struggling to put bread on the table."

Lindsay turned and stalked toward her grandfather's desk, where she planted her fists on her hips.

"You really have to get past that. Fifteen years is long enough to hold a grudge."

Her grandfather's back straightened. "Yeah, but I remember it as if it was yesterday. That land had oil. We were sitting on a gold mine and didn't even know it. Somehow the Lockharts knew. They just knew it. And now look at them, richer than Midas, and lording it over everyone else!"

"You can't undo what's done. We have to move on and make the best of our lot in life."

"And that's my plan." Henry Kemp stood and walked around the desk, taking his granddaughter by the hands. "Mark my words, things are gonna change around here."

Lindsay's brows wrinkled, her eyes narrowing. "What do you mean?"

"I'm workin' on something." Old Man Kemp dropped her hands and spun away, his lips turned up in a ghost of a smile.

Wade moved around the tree and ducked behind a bush. If Henry saw him spying on him, he'd fire him on the spot.

The old man looked out the window, past the tree where Wade had been standing to something far beyond. "I'm going to make things happen that should have happened a long time ago."

"Gramps, you aren't planning something crazy, are you?"

The old man's lips pressed into a firm line. "I

ain't tellin', but it'll make things right around here. And about damn time."

Lindsay moved up beside her grandfather and laid a hand on his arm. "I don't like that you're keeping secrets from me."

"This is one I had to keep, darlin'." He patted her hand. "It's for your own good. There are people who might try to stop me."

Voices sounded from the bunkhouse.

Wade doubled back around the house and came in from the opposite side, his mind churning through all he'd heard.

Henry Kemp had a plan. Question was, did it involve killing Governor Lockhart?

Wade had to find the evidence, and fast, of previous attempts to kill the governor, before another attempt met with success.

Chapter Four

"Suppertime!" Lindsay called out from the kitchen. She carried the heavy platter of roast beef and potatoes to the table and set it in the middle, the fragrant onions and spices wafting up, assaulting her senses. She hadn't eaten since early that morning and the way her stomach churned now didn't bode well for a satisfying meal, no matter how well prepared.

The girls had eaten macaroni and cheese while she'd prepared the meal for the adults. They'd play in their room while the men discussed the day's progress and plans for the next. Sometimes Lacey and Lyric joined them when they had a special meal, but not tonight. Until Lindsay had the opportunity to tell Wade he was a father, the less he saw of them the better.

Her heart thudded against her ribs as boots clumped on the porch outside the open front door. The ranch workers knew to be on time for dinner if they wanted a heaping helping. If not for the garden, the milk cow and the side of beef they'd put in the freezer a few months ago, they'd be facing beans and cornbread every meal.

With the bank account down to nothing, Lindsay didn't know where she'd come up with money to buy pantry staples. They had run out of tea and flour and the coffee supply neared empty.

Gramps led the men into the dining room where they assembled around the table. Gramps stood at the head of the table, leaving a seat at his right for Lindsay. Frank aimed for the seat beside Lindsay, but Dusty beat him to it, resting his hand on the back of the chair, staking his claim.

Frank grabbed the seat across from Lindsay.

Gramps raised a hand. "Take the chair at the end, Frank. I want the Coltrane boy to sit here and fill me in on what he's been up to."

Frank's eyes narrowed, but he backed away, purposely bumping into Wade's shoulder as he passed him and took the seat at the end of the table. He plunked down.

Gramps's mouth tightened and he remained standing as did all the other men and Lindsay. "You know the routine, Dorian."

Frank's cheeks reddened and he climbed to his feet. "Damn stupid, if you ask me."

"I didn't, now, did I?" Gramps nodded at Lindsay.

The tension in the air was thick enough that Lindsay could cut it with a knife. How the hell could she sit through an entire meal across from Wade? She might as well forget about eating. With her head bowed, she quietly asked the Lord's blessing for the food. As the men all muttered a rumbling amen, she added a silent prayer for help in handling this latest of crises on the Long K Ranch.

Lindsay sat and the men all dropped into their chairs reaching for the nearest platter of food. Gramps served himself a portion of the roast beef and potatoes and offered to serve Wade at the same time. "How long has it been since you've been home, Wade?"

Lindsay could have answered her grandfather's question down to the year, days and hours. Her gaze crossed over the bowl of corn she was scooping onto her plate.

"Five years," Wade replied, his gaze meeting Lindsay's.

Lindsay broke the eye contact first, her cheeks burning. The last time Wade had been to the Long K Ranch, she'd been engaged to Dr. Cal Murphy, certain Wade Coltrane would never step foot in Freedom, Texas, again. When he'd left to join the Army, he'd said he never wanted to come back to this two-bit town.

Lindsay had moped around for years, praying he'd return. Her heart broke a little more with each passing day. One year passed, then another and she'd given up hope that Wade would come back for her.

Her friends encouraged her to date other men to

get Wade out of her system. Desperate to shake the depression, she'd gone along with them when they set her up on a blind date with the new doctor in town, Cal Murphy.

He'd been everything Wade hadn't. Cal had a calming effect on her, where Wade stirred her blood and made her heart race. Cal was easy to date, demanding little from her, and not pushing sex. Wade made every female hormone in Lindsay's body light up like fireworks.

When Cal had asked her to marry him, it seemed like the natural progression. She said yes, knowing deep down that her heart still belonged to another.

Then Wade had blown into town on leave from the military. He'd been angry about her engagement, they'd argued out by the barn, she'd ridden off in a huff on her favorite mare.

Wade had followed.

He'd declared his love, swept her off her feet and they'd made love long into the night.

Not until the cool mist of dawn did Lindsay realize her mistake. She'd made love to Wade while engaged to another man. Guilt made her sick to her stomach. Angry at herself and at Wade for confusing her, she'd told Wade to go away and never come back.

A little over five years ago...

"Didn't you join the Army?" Gramps asked.

Wade jabbed a fork into his food, but didn't bother to lift it to his lips. "Yes, sir."

"What were you, Infantry?"

"No, sir. Special Forces." Wade pushed his food around, his jaw tightening.

Lindsay didn't have to avoid his gaze; Wade didn't look up from his food as Gramps asked questions. Why so evasive? He'd been so proud to be a member of the Army and that he'd been selected to be a part of the Special Forces.

He'd been deployed to Iraq when he'd left Freedom five years ago. Had his deployment changed all that? Had it changed Wade?

Lindsay allowed herself to study him for the first time since he'd returned.

Wade Coltrane had always been lean and muscular. Although his shoulders were broader, he seemed even thinner than usual, the shadows beneath his eyes, the scar over the right eyebrow and a nick in the curl of his ear were new. How had he gotten those? Had he been injured by a roadside bomb?

Her heart squeezed in her chest. All those years she hadn't received news of his exploits. With no family left in Freedom, news about Wade dried up.

Had he found another woman? Someone who would have worried about him, sat with him in the hospital and held his hand through the nightmare of recovery? Or had Wade been on his own like he'd been since his father's death when he was only seventeen?

"I was in the Army once," Frank boasted from the other end of the table. "Fighting a losing war over there in the Middle East. Damn waste of time. Just need to nuke them all and be done with it."

"That your answer to any difficult situation, Frank?" Dusty asked. "Nuke 'em?"

Frank shrugged. "Beats standing around in boots in one-hundred-and-thirty-degree temps."

"You can't blow things up and expect everything to work out in the end," Lindsay said. "Killing doesn't resolve anything."

"No, but it makes you feel a whole lot better, don't it?" Frank laughed. When nobody else did, he frowned and muttered, "It's an eye for an eye. Don't you believe in payback?"

Gramps slammed his hand on the table. "Hell, yeah, I'd like to dish out a little payback."

Lindsay cringed. *Here he goes again.* Not a day went by her grandfather didn't moan about the greatest wrong ever done to him.

"Wouldn't be hurtin' for money if the Lockharts hadn't stolen our oil," the old man grumbled.

"Gramps, they didn't steal our oil. They bought that land from you. They didn't discover oil on it until later."

"One year later." Gramps snorted. "Practically gave them that land."

"And we needed the money." She handed Gramps the platter of roast beef, hoping he'd change the subject. "Have some more supper, Gramps."

Wade looked up from his plate. "On my way through town this morning, I heard Lila Lockhart was involved in an accident last night."

Lindsay wanted to throw something at Wade. He knew the score. He'd lived here as a child. He knew how enraged her grandfather got at the mention of the Lockharts. Why feed the fire with more tinder?

"Serves her right." Her grandfather snorted. "Goin' around like royalty with money that should have been mine. Probably driving too fast, no respect for the speed limits the rest of us have to follow."

"They said someone booby-trapped the road with horseshoe nails." Wade looked directly at Gramps with piercing blue eyes.

Her grandfather harrumphed. "Might have thrown a few myself if I'd thought of it first."

"Gramps!" Lindsay slammed her fork down and shoved to her feet so fast that she almost toppled her chair. She'd had enough. The stress of sitting at the same table with Wade had finally gotten to her. Her grandfather's rant on the Lockharts just tipped her over the edge. "Excuse me while I go anywhere I don't have to listen to this nonsense."

Her grandfather clamped a hand on her arm. "Oh, Lindsay, girl, calm yourself down. I'll quit talkin' about those yahoos. Sit."

Wade sat at the other side of the table, a hint of a smile tweaking the corners of his mouth. He was laughing!

Heat boiled up her neck into her cheeks. Lindsay shook Gramps's hand off her arm. "I love you, Gramps, but I can't sit here another minute."

She took her plate and stormed out of the dining room. In the kitchen, she went to work cleaning the pots and pans she'd used preparing the meal. Scrubbing at the baked-on food did little to work off the anger and frustration that had built throughout the day.

How dare he come back now? And why? Obviously Wade hadn't come back because of the girls—he hadn't even recognized them as possibly being his own.

Her hands paused, buried in soapy water. Both girls had his black hair and blue eyes. After delivering them she'd gazed down at her baby daughters, ecstatic and heartsick at the same time. They'd been the spitting image of their father even then.

No wonder she'd never gotten over him. She saw him every day in Lacey and Lyric.

Hands reached around her and dropped plates into the soapy water.

The hair on the back of Lindsay's neck stood on end. The scent of soap, leather and denim let her know the man foremost in her thoughts stood close behind her. His breath stirred the hair curling against the side of her neck.

Her pulse sped, her breathing became labored. If she moved just a little, her back would touch his chest. He could wrap his arms around her and hold her in his warm embrace. The years would fall away, they'd be that happy couple making love into the night.

And pigs could learn to fly.

Lindsay dropped the pan she'd been scrubbing, soapsuds splashing over the sides of the sink. She ducked around Wade and reached for the dry towel hanging from the oven handle. "What do you want, Wade?"

"I came in here to help wash dishes."

"I don't need your help washing dishes."

"Then let me dry." He closed the distance between them, reaching out.

As if her body had its own ideas, she swayed toward his outstretched hand.

He snatched the towel from her fingers, twirled it and popped her hip.

"Ouch!"

"You know you hate doing dishes." That sexy smile that had always made her toes curl, tipped his lips upward. Although the trim beard hid a lot of his face, it couldn't hide the sparkle in his eyes.

Lindsay steeled herself from reacting to his charm. "Not as much as I hate someone helping me."

He didn't budge. "You used to love it when I helped in the kitchen."

Lindsay grabbed a glass from the dish drainer and plunked it into a cabinet just to keep busy, to focus on something other than the man she'd hung all her dreams on only to be disappointed time and again. "We were kids."

"Not so much."

She spun toward him, her fists clenching to keep from touching him. "Okay, we were young and stupid."

"We used to have a lot of fun." He whipped the towel around her, caught the other end and yanked her against him. "Remember this move?"

Her breasts pressed into his chest, her heart slamming against her rib cage, threatening to beat right out of her chest. "No," she said, her mouth inches from his. God, she could still feel the warmth of his lips on hers, kissing her as she lay naked in the starlight with him.

"Let me remind you." He leaned closer, his mouth descending to hers.

A plate clattered in the dining room, the noise snapping Lindsay out of the stupor and back to sanity. She shoved Wade away. "If you want to help do the dishes, you do them. I have other work that can be done."

She passed Gramps on her way out of the kitchen. She pointed a finger at him as she hurried away. "We need to talk after I get the girls down for the night. Don't you go off to bed until we do."

"Yes, ma'am," Gramps replied. "What's got your knickers in a twist, girl?"

Lindsay didn't bother to answer. She needed someone to hug. Two someones who loved her unconditionally. She needed that hug now.

For the next hour, she coaxed the girls through their baths and into their pajamas. After they cleaned up their toys, all three of them settled in Lyric's bed to read a story. It was Lyric's night to choose. She chose *Beauty and the Beast.*

Almost too jittery to sit still, Lindsay forced calm into her voice. Before long she was immersed in the story, the girls leaning against her shoulders, eyes wide and wondering. Never mind they'd heard the same story at least fifty times before.

Lindsay loved her girls and would do anything to make them happy. Would it make them happy to know about their father?

WADE KNEW exactly what Lindsay had wanted to say to her grandfather and he got way ahead of her by reminiscing with the old guy as they shared the task of cleaning up the kitchen. Apparently Wade looked enough like his father that Henry Kemp automatically trusted him.

That worked in Wade's favor, considering he was

there to build trust and find evidence. He pushed aside the gnawing guilt at betraying the man who'd opened his home to him when his father had passed away.

Old Man Kemp had always been gruff, but he'd also been fair in his treatment of his employees. When it came to his granddaughter, he'd declared her hands off to the ranch hands. That included Wade.

They'd managed to keep their secret flirtation just that…a secret while Wade and Lindsay were in high school.

Deep down Wade always knew he was the hired help and Lindsay was in a different class altogether. That's why he'd left to join the Army. He'd hoped to build a career for himself, prove he was worthy and then come back to ask her to marry him.

The idea had been a boy's romantic dream. The reality had kicked him in the teeth.

As Henry stacked the last clean plate in the cupboard, he sighed. "I'm glad you're here, Wade. The place hasn't been the same since your father passed."

"Nothing stays the same." Wade dried his hands and laid the towel over the oven handle. "Sometimes things need to change in order to get better."

"You got a point there." Henry stretched and rolled his shoulders. "I ain't gettin' much younger, but I got plans to get this place going again. The

Lockharts might have got the better of me once, but it won't happen again."

"How so?"

Henry shook his head. "I ain't a tellin'. You'll just have to wait and see, like the rest of them." He strode toward the hallway. "Could you find my granddaughter and tell her I'm ready to go to bed. If she wants to talk, it better be soon."

"Yes, sir."

With the old man's permission, Wade could walk through the house, searching for Lindsay. While he was at it, he'd look for anything that could be used as evidence that the old man was responsible for the most recent attack on Governor Lockhart.

Henry Kemp made no bones about his hatred for the Lockharts. He had the motivation to want to harm them. The question that tugged at Wade's conscience was, did Henry have the killer instinct?

Henry headed for his office, while Wade walked toward the rear of the house, down the hallway he remembered that led to Lindsay's bedroom. His groin tightened.

Back in high school, he'd sneaked into her room late one night when he'd been seventeen and she'd been sixteen. That was the night they'd both lost their virginity, the night he'd first declared his love to Lindsay Kemp.

Her bedroom door stood open, the lights off, the bed neatly made and empty. Although the room was empty, a soft voice carried through from somewhere inside.

Wade entered the room, the scent of Lindsay surrounding him, her presence filling the space. Everything about her room reminded him of Lindsay from the horse figurines she'd treasured as a child to the painting of a field of Texas bluebonnets that hung over her headboard.

Not much had changed in the room except the photographs of her daughters lining her dresser. He paused to stare at one picture of Lindsay and her twins, laughing in the sunlight, the love and joy reflected in their smiles made his chest ache.

Had he stayed in Freedom, would he have been a part of Lindsay's life? He shook his head. Probably not. The hired help didn't mix with the boss's family. Not then and not now. Lindsay deserved better.

The voice continued on. Lindsay's voice. He paused in front of what had once been Lindsay's closet. It had been remodeled into a doorway into the room beside Lindsay's.

A light shone down beside twin beds. Lindsay sat in the middle of one with a daughter nestled against either side.

Their dark hair spilled across the sheets, their faces soft and angelic, eyes closed.

Lindsay's voice faded off as she smiled down at them. She laid the book on the nightstand and stroked their hair several times before she slipped out of the bed and reached down to move one of the girls.

Wade cleared his throat softly, announcing his presence.

Lindsay jumped, her eyes widening, then narrowing.

Wade crossed the threshold into the little girl's room. "Let me."

"I can get her," Lindsay whispered.

He ignored her protest, scooping his hand beneath the little one and lifting. Light as kitten, the little girl rolled into his arms and snuggled against his chest. The scent of baby shampoo invaded his senses. Her silky, soft hair tickled his arm and everything about the little girl filled Wade with longing for something he could never have.

Lindsay turned back the covers on the other bed and moved aside.

Wade laid the child down on the bed and tucked her feet beneath the sheets.

Lindsay took over, adjusting the pillow beneath her head and drawing the blanket up under her chin, then pressing a kiss to the girl's forehead. When she'd finished, she returned to the other bed and performed the same ritual.

A lump the size of Texas lodged in Wade's throat. He could barely remember his mother, but the memories he did have involved a goodnight kiss just like the one Lindsay gave her daughters. "You're a good mother."

Lindsay switched the light off beside the bed and motioned Wade toward the door.

With one last glance at the sleeping children, he left the room. A sudden need for fresh air pushed him down the hall. Not until he was almost back to the dining room did he remember his initial task.

Wade conducted an about-face and bumped into Lindsay who had followed him. He grabbed her arms to keep her from falling, his fingers sliding across her skin, the urge to draw her closer so powerful that he shook with the effort to resist. "Your grandfather wanted to talk to you," he gritted out between clenched teeth.

"We need to talk," she said at the exact same time. "What?"

The green of her eyes drew him in, mesmerizing him, the curve of her full lower lip begged to be kissed. Wade swallowed hard on the rise of desire. He hadn't come to the Long K Ranch to rekindle a burned-out flame. His mission was to expose this woman's grandfather for attempted murder.

With all the self-control he could muster, his hands dropped to his sides, his fingers still tingling with her warmth. "Your grandfather said that if you want to talk to him, hurry up. He'd like to go to bed."

She pulled that full bottom lip between her teeth and chewed on it like she always had when she worked a problem in her head. "Okay, but we really need to talk."

"Tomorrow." Wade turned and left before he forgot why he'd come. Before he started thinking there might still be something between them, if he gave it a chance.

He should have learned long ago that he didn't deserve the boss's granddaughter. Even less so now. A man who could betray his unit had no business dreaming about a life with Lindsay and her little girls. They deserved better.

Wade stepped out on the porch and dragged in a deep breath, which did nothing to relieve the pain in his chest. As a high school kid, he'd been a dreamer. He'd long passed the dreams. Time to get on with life and accomplish this mission as soon as possible.

He dropped down off the front porch and rounded the side of the house, headed for the bunkhouse. The rattle of leaves in the bushes near the back of the house caught his attention. Wade dropped into a low crouch and eased toward the sound.

A shadowy figure rose above the bushes, leaning close to the same window Wade had stood near before dinner. The window to Henry Kemp's office.

Muffled voices carried through the glass—Henry and Lindsay arguing. Probably over his employment at the ranch.

Who would eavesdrop on their conversation? What did he hope to gain?

Before he could get any closer, the voices stopped and the light in the office window blinked out.

The figure remained standing near the window for another minute, then he pushed through the bushes and headed for the bunkhouse.

By the swagger in the man's walk, Wade could tell who it was.

Frank.

Anger burned in Wade's blood and his fists clenched.

Peeping Tom or real threat?

Given Frank's aggressive behavior with Lindsay earlier today, Wade leaned toward threat. He'd definitely keep an eye on that one.

Chapter Five

After a sleepless night tossing and turning, Lindsay got up at dawn and went to work preparing breakfast for the ranch hands. She missed the days when they could afford a cook and housekeeper.

She spent so much of her time cooking, cleaning and taking care of the house when she'd rather be working with the horses and cattle. As a child she'd participated in every roundup. She'd mended fences alongside her grandfather and ridden every inch of the Long K Ranch at least a hundred times.

Since the girls' birth, her range had been curtailed unless she had them in the mother's day-out program at the Cradles to Crayons Daycare.

Not that she minded. She preferred to be involved in their lives. And now that they were bigger, they could help out by fetching and carrying. Hard work hadn't hurt her growing up. In fact, it had made her stronger, able to handle every curveball life had to throw at her.

Well, almost every one. Losing Wade had been

the hardest to handle, but she'd survived, and now she had her two girls to consider.

After she set the platters of food on the sideboard, she escaped to her suite of rooms to gather laundry. If she was honest with herself, she'd admit she was avoiding the men. One man. Wade Coltrane.

She needed to talk to him but wanted to time it right. Telling a man he had two four-year-old daughters wasn't something you blurted out over coffee and scrambled eggs. It had to be the right setting and the right time.

When she'd finished gathering dirty clothes, straightening beds and putting away toys, Lindsay stood in the middle of her bedroom, her eyes closed, her head tilted back. The right timing would have been over five years ago when she found out she was pregnant.

"Mommy, are you praying?" Lacey tugged at her hand.

"Are you talking to God?" Lyric slipped her fingers into Lindsay's other hand.

She opened her eyes and grinned. Her girls made her life not only bearable, but they also filled her with joy each passing minute. "Yes, babies."

"Did you ask him to make Joey's turtle better?" Lyric stared up at Lindsay, her forehead wrinkled in a frown.

Lindsay squatted beside her girls, gathering them into her arms. "You bet."

"We're hungry." Lacey dragged her toward the door.

Her heart in her throat, Lindsay let the girls pull her toward the dining room.

Gramps was picking up his plate and carrying it to the kitchen. "You missed the men. They ate and left to get out to the north forty. Gonna bring that herd of steers closer for roundup next week."

Lindsay let out the breath she'd been holding. Not only had she avoided running into Wade at breakfast, but she could also postpone the confrontation all day. "You be careful out there today, Gramps. It's gonna be a scorcher. The girls and I will be working the corral today."

"Good. It needs to be done or we'll have a heck of a time loading." Gramps's brows knit. "Maybe I should leave one of the men to help you. That gate can be pretty cantankerous. We want everything ready when we bring the trucks in to load the cattle going to market."

Lindsay's heart skipped a beat and she forced what she hoped was a reassuring smile to her face. "Don't change a thing. You need the men out on the range. I can manage on my own. I'll have my little helpers with me."

Her grandfather grinned down at his great-granddaughters. "Leave the heavy liftin' until we get back."

"Will do. You better get going or they'll leave without you." She herded her grandfather toward the door and stood on the porch until all five men galloped out of the barnyard for a full day of moving cattle.

Her gaze followed Wade's tall figure, riding as though he was one with the horse. He sat straight in the saddle, his cowboy hat slung low over his forehead.

Were his shoulders broader? The beard made him darker, more mysterious and horribly sexy. Lindsay found herself wondering what it would feel like against her skin. A flush of heat spread through her body that had nothing to do with the rising heat of the day.

Lacey and Lyric raced around the side of the house screaming and laughing.

"Come on, girls, we have work to do on the corral." Lindsay gathered her tool belt, clipped it around her hips, settled a straw cowboy hat on her head and headed for the barn.

She worked for several hours, yanking off old rotten boards. Thank goodness she'd found a stack of unused boards in the loft last week or they'd have had to do with the rotten railing. It was bad enough she'd had to spend grocery money to purchase new hinges for the gate, the old ones having rusted clean through.

Lacey and Lyric helped by bringing boards to her as she needed them. They struggled, but they were determined to help. Stubborn like their mother... and their father.

Nearing noon, Lindsay stood beside the last panel, yanking old nails from the wood.

The girls brought a board from the stack by the gate, perspiration curling the hair that had escaped their ponytails. They bent to lay the board on the ground beside their mother.

Lyric straightened and brushed the dust from her little hands. "Joey helps his daddy build things."

"We're helping our mommy." Lacey planted her hands on her hips.

Lacey climbed up on the panel beside the one Lindsay worked on. "Where's our daddy?"

"Do we have a daddy?" Lyric climbed up beside Lacey.

Lindsay had been dreading this question ever since the girls were born. All they knew about families was that they had a mother and a grandfather. Until they started going to Cradles to Crayons, they hadn't been too exposed to other children whose daddies picked them up.

For years, she'd planned on telling them that their daddy lived somewhere else, that he loved them but couldn't come to see them. As she opened her mouth to feed them the canned answer, her words clogged her throat. How could she lie to them when their father lived in the bunkhouse and he'd probably be a great father to his girls?

If he knew they were his.

"I'll give you that answer another day, ladies. Right now I have work to do and I could use a big ol' cup of water. Think you two can go up to the house and come back with water for the three of us?"

"Yes!" Lacey leaped off the railing and was half-way up to the house by the time Lyric reached the ground.

Lyric stood looking at her mother. "For Christmas can we have a daddy?"

"Come on, Lyric!" Lacey shouted.

Those blue eyes bored a hole right through Lindsay's soul.

"We'll see, Lyric." Lindsay tousled her daughter's dark ponytail. "Who knows what Santa has for good little girls."

Her eyes glazed with unshed tears, Lindsay turned back to the task of nailing the new board onto the corral fence. "You better catch up with your sister before she reaches the kitchen," she called over her shoulder, afraid to face her daughter in case she asked about the moisture in her eyes.

Lyric ran off, her black hair falling free of the ponytail.

A tear slipped out the corner of Lindsay's eye, followed by another and another. Soon a river of tears slipped down Lindsay's face. She scrubbed at them with her shirtsleeve, unaware of the hoofbeats until a horse charged into the barn yard.

Quickly, she scrubbed the remaining wetness from her face and looked up through watery eyes at the man she'd been crying about.

He dropped down to the ground and strode to her side. "What's wrong?"

"Nothing." Damned if she didn't hiccup, which inspired still more sobs to rise up her throat and choke off her air.

"Liar." Wade reached out with both hands and brushed the tears from her cheeks with his thumbs, pushing the cowboy hat to the back of her head to see her better. "Kemps don't cry."

"Exactly."

"So what are these?" He scooped a fat tear from her cheek and held it out as evidence.

"I hammered my thumb." She held up her uninjured thumb. What else could she do? She couldn't hold out her heart. "I'm allowed a little pain, aren't I?"

"Come here." He opened his arms.

Despite every rational thought screaming at her to walk away, Lindsay couldn't stop herself. Since he'd shown up yesterday, every fiber of her being yearned for him.

She swayed toward him until her forehead rested against his chest, her face buried in his black T-shirt. Her cowboy hat tipped off her head and fell to the dust behind her.

Arms like iron bands circled around her, pulling her closer. The scents of leather, dust and male musk assailed her nostrils, that uniquely Wade smell that had always made her heart beat faster. She pressed even closer, her fingers curling into the jersey knit of his shirt, soaking in his warmth and strength, wishing she could stand there forever.

Squealing laughter brought her back to her senses and she jumped back, out of his arms.

Lacey ran ahead of Lyric, both carrying plastic cups of water, spilling most of it as they ran.

"What do we have here?" Wade asked.

"We brought Mommy a drink of water," Lacey slid to a stop and held out her cup.

Lyric ground to a halt a little late, the water in her cup sloshing over onto Wade.

Once again, Lindsay held her breath, waiting for the other shoe to drop and Wade to realize these miniature replicas of him were his daughters.

"You can give yours to Mommy. I'll give mine to Mr. Wade." Lyric shoved her cup toward Wade.

His jeans soaked where Lyric spilled the water. Wade graciously accepted the offering.

Lindsay took the proffered cup from Lacey and drank the tepid water, glad for any liquid at this point and the distraction.

"Can we play in the garden, Mommy? Please?" Lacey asked, jumping up and down.

"Please?" Lyric added her voice to Lacey's.

"As long as you don't play in the tomatoes. Last time you played in the garden, you ruined half a tomato plant."

"I get the red truck!" Lacey ran for the garden plot off to the side between the house and the barn, still within sight of the corral.

"We won't play in the tomatoes," Lyric promised, racing after her sister.

"Watch for snakes and don't touch them!" Lindsay sighed.

"They remind me of you when you were that little."

Lindsay wanted to argue that they didn't look anything like her, but she clamped her lips closed and faced off with Wade. "Why did you come back?"

"Your grandfather was worried you'd try to tackle mending the gate without help."

"No, why did you come back to Freedom? To the Long K Ranch?"

"I needed work and the Long K Ranch is the only job I know outside the military."

"Gramps has some warped sense of karma or something and thinks you're going to bring us good luck. I told him we couldn't afford to pay you, but he insisted on keeping you here."

Wade's lips twisted. "Glad to know you fought for me, even if it was to get me fired."

"You really should find another place to work. We're broke, the cattle sale next week may be a bust the way cattle prices have fallen since the drought began. I don't know where we'll get the money for this week's payroll. You're destined to find another job, why not start now, rather than work for an empty paycheck?"

"Nice speech, but no. I'm staying." Wade laughed.

"Let's just say I like rooting for the underdog. This place can work if you have faith."

"And an unlimited bankroll, both of which I'm a little light on right now." She reached down to retrieve her hat, slapping it against her jean-clad leg.

"Tsk, tsk." Wade took the hat from her fingers and deposited it on her head. "You will never give up on this ranch. It's part of your life, your heritage."

"My albatross." She sighed. "You're right, though. It's home. To me, the girls and Gramps. I'd hate to lose it."

"How bad is it?"

"Bad enough." She lifted her hammer. "Now, if you'll excuse me, I have a gate to mend before I start supper for the hands."

"That's why your grandfather sent me back. To help you with the fence, so move over."

"I don't need your help."

"I didn't ask you if you did. I'm being paid to help. Quit arguing and let me help. It'll get done a lot faster."

Lindsay clamped her lips shut and went to work. The faster they got the gate done, the quicker she could get away from Wade and all the temptation he represented.

She'd thought she was well over the guy. Boy, had she been wrong. Throughout the afternoon, she opened her mouth to tell him about the girls, but each time, she'd bit down on the confession, internally claiming that the timing wasn't right. Hell, the timing would never be right, she'd have to pluck up the courage and just do it.

After supper when they would be not so sweaty and maybe alone.

WADE WORKED alongside Lindsay through the afternoon. Every direction he turned, she was there, her body close enough to touch, her hands brushing against his as they maneuvered the heavy wooden gate to set the new hinges in place.

The more he worked with Lindsay, the more he realized he couldn't work at the ranch without touching her again. His life had gone sour since she'd told him to leave the last time; why drag her into the quagmire it had become?

Apparently Lindsay had enough to worry about without Wade confusing her with unwanted attention.

The ranch had financial troubles. Henry Kemp made no bones about blaming the Lockharts for his money woes. What better motivation for wanting to do harm to the governor?

A relationship with the granddaughter of the man he was spying on was completely out of the question. But Wade couldn't stop wishing for what couldn't be, no matter how pathetic and impossible it was.

He couldn't do this assignment. Being around Lindsay pushed him past his limits.

Working in silence, they completed the task.

"After I feed the horses, pigs and milk the cow, I'll start supper. It should be ready in about an hour and a half."

"I'll take care of the animals out here. It's getting late, the men will be coming in soon and wanting their supper."

"You sure?"

"I know what to do. Go."

She turned toward the house, her shoulders sagging.

Wade wished he could do more, but the woman was stubborn.

A full day's work and then preparing a meal for five hungry men…she had to be exhausted.

Although Wade told himself he didn't care, he knew it was a lie. He did care. Too much.

"Lindsay."

She looked back over her shoulder.

"Don't fix me anything, I'll eat dinner in town. I have an errand to run."

Her brow wrinkled and he could tell she wanted to ask him about his errand. Wade didn't offer an explanation, nor would he if she asked.

After a shower in the bunkhouse, Wade climbed into his truck and headed for Freedom. If all went as planned, he'd be reassigned by morning and wouldn't have to see Lindsay Kemp ever again.

THIRTY MINUTES LATER, standing in front of Bart Bellows, Wade held his hat in his hand. "You got the wrong man for this job, Mr. Bellows."

The seventy-two-year-old man, with his balding fringe of hair and beard, leaned back in his wheelchair behind the massive mahogany desk, his piercing blue eyes boring a hole right through Wade's excuses. "Why do you think that?"

"I used to live at that ranch. I know Old Man Kemp and his granddaughter. It just doesn't seem right to be spying on them."

"You know them. For that reason and given your Special Forces specialty for infiltrating enemy lines, you're the perfect man for the job."

"Can't you find anyone else to do it?"

"I got all my men assigned to other missions. I need you at the Long K Ranch."

"I'll do anything else, just find someone to fill my spot."

Bart tapped his pen on the desk. "Tell you what. Stay on for at least another couple days and I'll see what I can do."

A groan rose in Wade's throat. He swallowed hard to keep it from sounding out loud. He owed Bart a lot for bringing him on board with Corps Security and Investigations. Before Bart's call, he'd been wandering from job to job, no purpose in life. The Army Special Forces had been his life, his identity, his reason for being until he'd been captured and tortured in a Taliban terrorist camp.

The familiar ache in his chest intensified. Bart had given him this chance to prove he wasn't a failure, that he could be trusted to accomplish the mission. A chance to start over.

Wade plunked his cowboy hat on his head and squared his shoulders. "I'll stay. And I'll get that evidence you need. Then I want out."

"Deal. All we need is the evidence to stop who-ever is responsible for the attacks on Governor Lockhart. She's a good woman. She deserves our best effort."

With a nod, Wade left Bart's office. He climbed into his pickup and drove into Freedom, hunger gnawing at his insides. Still early evening, the lights on the Talk of the Town Restaurant shone out into the street. Cars and trucks lined the small parking lot and people entered and left.

He'd eaten there once and the food had been decent. Wade pulled into the parking lot next to what looked like one of the trucks from the Long K Ranch. For a moment, he hesitated with his fingers on the keys. What were the chances Lindsay Kemp had come to town this late?

Slim to none. She had the girls at home to think about. Probably reading a book to them now, get-ting them ready to go to sleep. His chest hurt with that familiar ache. When he'd come back to Free-dom five years ago, he'd come to ask Lindsay to marry him. He'd had images of them being together, maybe raising a couple kids.

He switched off his truck engine.

Dreams had no place in his life right now. His

mission was to collect evidence to put away the man who was responsible for hiring Rory Stockett to shoot the governor. The same man who'd booby-trapped the road to Lila Lockhart's estate.

Part of infiltrating and investigating was blending in and listening to the locals. With his dark coloring, his beard and his grasp of languages, he'd fit right in with the Afghani tribes, forming relationships with the tribe leaders and local clerics.

How hard would it be to gain the confidence of locals here in Freedom? He spoke the same language, he'd lived here most of his young life and he already knew quite a few of the people.

Wade climbed down from the truck and entered the Talk of the Town. People filled half the seats around the tables. The empty tables had dirty dishes from recently departed patrons.

A young woman, with her hair pulled back in a ponytail, hurried from table to table cleaning as fast as she could. "Take a seat wherever you like. I'll be with you in a minute," she called out as she dumped plates and glasses into the big plastic tub she carried.

Wade took a seat at a dirty table in a far corner, his back to the wall, facing the entry.

The young woman cleared the table, wiped it clean and ran for the swinging door into the kitchen. In a moment, she returned, her hands damp, perspiration beading on her forehead, pulling a tablet and pencil from her apron. "Hi, sorry, I'm Faith.

It's been in a rush and one of my waitresses called in sick. What can I get you?"

Wade ordered a chicken fried steak, mashed potatoes and green beans.

Faith hurried off, promising to bring coffee as soon as she could.

As he waited for his order, his gaze panned the interior of the restaurant. He recognized a few of the older people. Some of the ones closer to his age looked familiar from high school, but he wasn't completely sure due to possible hair loss and added pounds.

Henry Kemp emerged from the men's room and took a seat with his back to Wade at a table with two of his cronies, Fred March and Stan Lorry. They sat a couple tables over, but he could hear every word they said as loud as they spoke.

A young woman with brown hair and blue eyes entered.

Faith waved from across the restaurant. "Hey, Chloe. Good to see you."

Wade recognized the latest customer as Governor Lockhart's youngest daughter, a journalist, with a wicked sense of politics based on her articles.

"Have a seat at the counter, I'll be right with you."

Henry Kemp stared over at the girl, his eyes narrowing. "I tell you, the Lockharts are the reason the Long K Ranch is in such a hellhole now. If they hadn't stolen that oil from me, I'd be sitting fat and happy, not a care in the world, like them." He spoke loud enough that the woman at the counter couldn't help but hear the reference to her family. She glanced over her shoulder, her brows raised, but she had the good sense not to jump into the conversation.

"I thought the Lockharts bought that property." Fred lifted his cup of coffee and sipped.

"They did, but they knew." Henry spoke to Fred, but his glance swung to Chloe again.

"Knew what?" Stan asked.

"They knew when they bought it that it had so much oil beneath those acres they'd be richer than King Midas as soon as they closed the deal."

"It was over a year after they bought it that they discovered oil."

"You think they didn't have some oil speculator out there checkin' things out before they signed the sale papers?" Henry snorted. "Damn Lockharts would just as soon cheat you as look you in the eye and spit."

Chloe's back stiffened and she rose slowly from the bar stool at the counter.

Faith stopped to pat her friend's hand. "Don't lower yourself to his level," she said. Wade could barely hear her words, but he read her lips as they moved.

Fred continued the conversation. "Ran into Lila Lockhart at the farmer's market the other day. She seemed right nice to me."

"Well, she ain't." Henry thumped his empty coffee mug on the table. "And she ain't got a chance in hell of a return trip to the governor's mansion in Austin."

"Why?" Stan glanced across at Chloe, his brows furrowed in a worried frown.

Henry smiled like the cat that ate the canary. "I don't think she'll live that long."

Stan Lorry shot a quick glance at Chloe and looked back at Henry, leaning close to his old friend. "You ought not say things like that in public. Next thing you know, they'll be charging you with hiring that fella that took a potshot at the governor right here in this restaurant a couple weeks ago."

"I ain't hired no hit man, if that's what you're saying. If I did, I'd be sure I got me a good one that didn't miss."

"That's it. I can't take this anymore." Chloe stood, her jaw clenched, her eyes narrowed.

Faith pressed her cell phone into Chloe's hand. "Call this number, while I conduct a little damage control."

Wade hoped Faith wouldn't stop the old man quite yet. He leaned closer. Henry Kemp had always been blustery and loud, but he usually didn't mean anyone harm. Could he have hired the hit man who had taken a potshot at Lila Lockhart? If he had, surely he wouldn't be talking about it in such a public forum. Wade listened carefully just in case the old man let something slip.

"That Lila Lockhart ain't gonna win the next election if I have anything to do with it," Old Man Kemp continued. "She doesn't deserve to be governor of this fine state and she has no business running for a public office as corrupt as she is. She and her family stole my oil, I tell you."

Faith marched across the tile floor and stopped at Henry's table. "Mr. Kemp, I'm gonna have to ask you to keep it down. You're disturbing the other customers."

Henry's brows furrowed. "I don't care who hears me. They need to know what a crook that Lila Lockhart is."

Faith planted her free fist on her hip. "Not in my restaurant."

The old man's face reddened and he opened his mouth to say something else when Lindsay entered, Lyric and Lacey in tow, both wearing their pajamas and wiping sleep from their eyes.

"Gramps, are you disturbing the peace again?" Lindsay stomped across the floor and stood over her grandfather. "It's time to come home."

"You're my granddaughter, not my wife. I'll come home when I'm good and ready. I got me a bone to pick with this young lady here."

"You're done picking bones. Pay your bill and let's go." She hooked his elbow and practically lifted him from his chair.

Lacey tugged at Lindsay's shirt. "I'm tired, Mommy."

"Me, too," Lyric echoed. "Why won't Gramps come home?"

"Because he's being a stubborn old coot." She glared down at her grandfather. "Are you going to keep your great-granddaughters awake being stubborn?"

"Go home. I don't know why you dragged them out this late anyhow."

"I'm not going home without you. Girls, pull up a chair, we'll wait until Gramps sees fit to leave."

Wade grinned as the girls pushed chairs toward the table with the three old men.

Lindsay Kemp had a temper and was just as stubborn as her grandfather. He'd always admired her sense of justice. She didn't give up without a good fight.

The grin faded from his face and Wade almost stood to leave. She didn't give up without a fight.

He'd cracked under pressure of torture and given up information that could have gotten his men killed. What kind of man did that?

No kind of man. A dirt bag, weakling and traitor did stuff like that.

Henry Kemp rose from his chair, his mouth pressed into a thin line. "Since your mother doesn't see fit to take you home, guess I'll have to. Come on, girls."

Lyric and Lacey each grabbed a hand and walked their great-grandfather to the door, leaning against him.

Lindsay nodded at Fred and Stan. "Gentlemen, have a good evening."

They sat up straight, their hands coming up in a mock salute.

Faith smiled across at Lindsay and mouthed the words, "Thank you."

As she turned to leave, Lindsay spotted Wade in the corner. Her eyes widened, then narrowed. She didn't say anything as she left without another glance in his direction.

Just as well, what would she say? *Hey, Wade, why don't you and me conduct a repeat performance of our last reunion five years ago?*

He set down his fork and motioned for Faith to bring his bill. Suddenly he had no appetite. Between Henry Kemp's bluster and Lindsay's lack of interest, everything he'd managed to consume had knotted in his gut.

The sooner he left Freedom and the Long K Ranch the better. There was nothing left for him there; it wasn't home anymore. He'd be better off starting over somewhere else. Tomorrow, he'd find a way into Henry's study and find that damn evidence.

Chapter Six

Lindsay was still fuming when she got home. She'd insisted on driving, needing something to curl her fists around to keep from slamming them into the dash. When would her grandfather learn to keep his big mouth shut?

Henry Kemp sat in the passenger seat, grumbling all the way back to the ranch. At least he had the good sense not to argue while Lindsay drove.

The girls were asleep again in the backseat before they reached the ranch.

To her grandfather's credit, he had the decency to help her carry them in to their beds.

Once they had Lyric and Lacey tucked in, Lindsay followed her grandfather into the hallway.

"Gramps, we need to talk."

"Not now, girl. I'm tired and I have a full day tomorrow."

Not to be deterred, she moved in front of him. "This feud has got to stop."

"What feud?" Gramps pushed around her and

into his office. "You can't go around bad-mouthing the governor of the state of Texas."

"It's a free country. I can say what I want."

"Not when it can be construed as a threat to a governor." Lindsay perched on the edge of his desk. "If you're not careful, they'll start suspecting you of paying that man to shoot at Lila Lockhart or of putting those horseshoe nails on her road." Lindsay's eyes widened. "You didn't do those things, did you? Please, Gramps, tell me you didn't."

Gramps's lips pursed. "Of course, I didn't. But someone needs to teach that family a lesson."

"Not you, Gramps." Lindsay stood and wrapped her arms around her grandfather. "You and the girls are all I have left in this world. I couldn't stand it if something were to happen to you."

Her grandfather patted her back. "Now, Lindsay, girl. Ain't nothin' gonna happen to this old codger. Don't you go a worryin' none. Got enough on your plate as it is." He set her away from him. "Now I gotta get some shut-eye or I'll be dead on my feet in the morning."

Lindsay smiled. "Goodnight, Gramps. I love you."

"You know I love you, too." Her grandfather left the office, his boots tapping a pattern on the wood flooring down the hallway to his bedroom.

Too wound up to go to bed, Lindsay stepped out on the back porch and breathed in the cool night air. It never ceased to amaze her how chilly it could be at night when the days got so blazing hot.

Although moonless, the sky put on a showing of what seemed like every star in the universe to light the night, like a cloak of diamonds sparkling in the heavens.

Lindsay liked evenings like this. She used to lie outside on the ground with Wade identifying the constellations. Her gaze shot to the bunkhouse. There she went again, thinking about Wade Coltrane.

A horse whinnied in the barn, drawing her attention away from the bunkhouse. When the horse whinnied again, Lindsay stepped off the porch and walked to the barn to check on it. Probably just restless like her.

Lindsay rolled her shoulders in an attempt to relieve some of the stress of the day. Having Wade around made her feel edgy and out of sorts. She opened the door to the barn, switched on the light and stepped inside.

Sweetie Pie stuck her head over the top of her stall and whinnied.

"What's wrong, girl? Can't sleep, either?" Lindsay walked by Jimmy-B and Whiskers, stopping to rub Sweetie Pie's soft muzzle.

The sorrel mare nuzzled Lindsay's hand briefly, then tossed her head, shaking her mane.

"Got a mouse in there with you or something?" Lindsay leaned up on her toes to glance down into

Sweetie Pie's stall. Without a flashlight, she couldn't see the corners to know whether a mouse had come to munch on the grain the horse had dropped.

She dropped down on her feet and spun around and ran into a man. Lindsay almost screamed, her voice catching in her throat when she recognized who it was.

Frank Dorian.

Sweetie Pie whinnied and stamped her hoof in the dirt.

Lindsay seconded Sweetie Pie's assessment of the situation. As her grandfather would say, the best defense is always a good offense. "What are you doing in the barn at this time of night?"

Dorian shrugged. "I could ask you the same thing." His gaze traveled down over her face and lower to the V-neckline of her blouse.

"It's my barn. You didn't answer the question." She crossed her arms over her chest, refusing to be intimidated by Frank's blatant perusal of her body.

"Just checking on things. I thought I heard a noise."

"Well, I'll take care of it. You can go back to the bunkhouse."

"Why would I go and do that? The night is just starting to get interesting." He stepped closer to her and ran his hand down her bare arm.

Anger fired through her veins and she slapped Frank's hand away. Lindsay didn't back away, refusing to let Dorian get the better of her. "I thought I was clear yesterday that you were never to touch me again."

"You might be saying 'no' but your body is saying 'yes.'" He ran his other hand down her other arm.

"No, it isn't. Keep your hands off me or I'll break your fingers."

"How is it you act so tough but your skin is soft. I'd have thought it would be all leathery like your personality."

"Pack your bags, Dorian. I won't have you working here if you can't take orders from me."

"Like I said, you can't fire me. Your grandfather hired me."

"When I tell him that you're harassing me, he'll fire you on the spot."

"I wouldn't do that if I was you."

"But then you aren't me. Pack and get out of here."

"I think not." He stepped closer, his hands clamping down on her arms.

With her back against Sweetie Pie's stall, she didn't have much room to move, but she knew enough to get herself out of this situation.

Lindsay shoved her hands up through the middle of his arms, and to the sides, breaking his hold on her. Then she grabbed his pinky and snapped it at the base like breaking a twig off a tree branch.

Her stomach lurched, but she didn't lose the contents, she waited for his next move.

Dorian yelled and doubled over, clutching his finger with his other hand.

Lindsay took the opportunity to duck around him and brace herself for the next attack. Breaking a finger would either get it through his thick skull that she didn't want his attentions or just piss him off.

Lindsay guessed it would piss him off.

Frank straightened, the veins popping out on his face, his eyes narrowing into slits. "I'll kill you for that."

"I don't think today will be your lucky day." Lindsay opened her mouth to scream.

Before she could get the air past her vocal cords, Dorian lurched toward her, his good arm swinging in an air-splitting backhand.

She had just enough time to block the hit from connecting with her face, but the force slammed her backward and she fell to the ground. Not good. Lindsay scrambled, crab-crawling backward.

Frank's lips curled back in a snarl and he kicked at her, the toe of his boot glancing off her thigh.

Lindsay cried out, rolled to the side and sprang to her feet. She ran for the barn door but only got two steps before Frank's hand grasped her hair and yanked her backward.

Sweetie Pie, Jimmy-B and Whiskers screamed with her, pawing at their stall doors.

Frank's arm circled her waist and yanked her against his body, lifting her off the ground. His other hand clamped over her mouth and nose, cutting off her air.

She tried to bite his hand, but he held so tightly that she couldn't. The yellow glow of the overhead lights dimmed, growing gray and fuzzy around the edges as Lindsay's oxygen-deprived brain began shutting down.

WADE ARRIVED back at the ranch thirty minutes after Lindsay. He'd changed his mind and stayed longer at the café to eavesdrop on the gossip between Faith and Chloe. After Henry had gone, Chloe filled Faith in on the latest attempts on her mother's life and her own speculation about who might have done it.

Their conjecture centered on Henry and his blustering threat to get even with the Lockharts.

When talk turned to babies and weddings, Wade left, anxious to get back to the Long K Ranch. He wondered if Lindsay had encountered any more trouble from her grandfather.

Upon arrival, he noted the lights out in the house and assumed Lindsay had gone off to bed.

Tired to the bone, Wade tromped into the bunkhouse, stripped out of his clothes and stepped into the communal shower. As he soaped his body and washed his hair, thoughts of Lindsay slid over him with the suds.

She'd entered the café tonight like a woman on a mission, all determination and gritty. Her parents had died when she was only seven years old. For having been raised by her ill-tempered grandfather, she'd turned out all right.

But in the five years since he'd been home, some of the roles had reversed. Where Henry had called all the shots before, the new, improved Lindsay now laid down the law with her grandfather. She rode herd on his activities, using her daughters as leverage to break through any stubborn streak he threw her way.

Wade grinned as he recalled the fire in her moss-green eyes as she'd rounded up Henry and moved him out of the café as quickly as possible.

The smile faded as he realized the scenario had appeared to be a repeat performance, the parts played multiple times from Faith asking Chloe to call, to Lindsay arriving in time to pull her grandfather out of the café and make him go home.

As if Lindsay didn't already have her hands full with twin four-year-olds to care for.

As he shed the towel and reached for his boxers, Wade paused. Was that the sound of horses screaming? He tipped his head to the side.

Yes. And it was coming from the barn.

He yanked on his jeans and boots and ran for the door, making a note of Frank's empty bunk as he passed by. He'd called Bart while in town to get the skinny on Frank Dorian. The man had shown up several weeks ago, hiring on with the Long K

Ranch. No one knew much about him. Knowing Bart, he'd get the scoop before long.

The horses whinnied again, hooves banging against wood inside their stalls.

Wade sniffed the air for smoke, relieved he didn't detect any. What the hell had the horses spooked?

A woman's frightened scream shook him to the core and he burst through the barn door.

Frank Dorian had his back to the door, struggling with someone in his arms. He spun and shook the figure like a rag doll, red hair spilling out of his arm.

A wash of red, blood-searing rage flashed over Wade and he charged on Frank, yanking him around.

The man had his arm around Lindsay's middle, his hand over her mouth and nose. With both hands occupied, he couldn't defend his face against the fistful of knuckles Wade planted on his nose.

The man screamed like a girl and let go of Lindsay, his hand going to his nose, blood streaming through his fingers. "Son of a bitch!" He dropped his left shoulder and charged into Wade.

With a switch dodge to the side, Wade avoided the collision, and gave the man a shove from behind as he passed.

Unable to alter his course at the last minute, Frank rammed into a sturdy, oak six-by-six post head first. He went down like a sack of potatoes, crumpling to the ground in an ungainly heap.

Wade spun toward Lindsay, his pulse banging through his veins so hard that he couldn't hear for the rush of blood against his eardrums. Had he been too late? Had Frank killed her?

Lindsay pushed up from the ground to a sitting position, gulping air into her lungs.

Wade remembered to breathe, his heart racing to resume the flow of oxygen to his brain.

Behind him, Frank stirred and staggered to his feet.

His feet braced, fists clenched, ready for the fight, Wade faced him. "Get off the Long K Ranch and never show yourself here again. Got that?"

"Mr. Kemp—"

"Once he knows what you did to me," Lindsay said from her position on the ground, "he'll shoot your sorry carcass if you ever show your face around here again. Now leave before I call the sheriff and have you arrested for assault."

Dorian pressed his hand to stop the flow of blood from his nose. "You'll be sorry."

"The only thing I'm sorry about is that I didn't kick you off the ranch sooner." Lindsay jerked her head to the side. "Leave before I find a gun and shoot you myself."

Frank stared from Lindsay to Wade.

Wade glared at the man. "Do as she said, Dorian. She never misses."

His lip pulled back in a snarl, Frank stumbled

past Wade and Lindsay and disappeared through the barn door.

Lindsay's shoulders slumped and she smiled up at Wade, her lips trembling.

He lifted her to her feet and gently folded her into his arms. He wanted to hug her tightly to his chest and never let her go again, but he didn't know if she'd suffered any broken ribs. She needed all the air she could breathe after nearly being suffocated.

Lindsay leaned against him, warm breath brushing his skin, fingers clutching at his arms, her body shaking. "I had him where I wanted him, you know," she said.

It was just like Lindsay to make a joke of a really bad situation, but it was no less unexpected. Tension released in a rush and Wade chuckled. He pulled her closer, hugging her against him, laughing harder.

How long had it been since he'd laughed? How long had it been since he'd found anything to laugh about? This firecracker of a woman had always had a way of making him see reason, of finding the humor in a situation. She'd always shown him the power of living to the fullest, one day at a time.

As her citrusy scent wrapped around his senses, the laughter died and another emotion welled inside him so strongly that he could barely breathe.

Her hands against his skin burned through to his heart, making him want those things he knew he could never have. And knowing he couldn't have her made it all the more imperative he take what he could while he had her here in his arms.

When Lindsay's face turned up to his, reason flew out the door and he bent to capture her lips with his.

His mouth covered hers, his tongue tracing the line of her full, sensuous lips. He nibbled at the lower one, tugging it with his teeth. When she gasped, he swooped in to capture her tongue, thrusting deep, tasting her sweetness.

He'd been back from the Middle East for months, but he hadn't felt like he'd come home until now. Home had always been in this woman's arms.

Her fingers crept up his chest, her hands circling around the back of his neck, drawing him closer. She rubbed her cheek against his beard, a smile tilting the corners of her lips. "I like the beard, it makes you look dangerous."

Caught in a wave of desire so strong, Wade forgot about tomorrow, shoved the shadows of his past into the far corners of his memory and drowned in the here and now. He lifted Lindsay, wrapping her legs around his waist, and carried her to the hay stacked high against the far wall. He dropped her to her feet and reached for a clean horse blanket, spreading it on the cushion of loose straw.

For a moment Lindsay stood there, chewing her bottom lip.

Wade held his breath, sure she'd come to her

senses and run screaming from the barn, calling him all kinds of a creep for taking advantage of her after she'd just been attacked by another man.

Instead, she took his hand and drew him down to the blanket with her.

Bottle rockets could have gone off next to him, mortar shells exploded and a herd of wild horses could run through the barn and Wade wouldn't have been able to look away from the light burning in her green eyes.

Shaken loose from its ponytail, her wild, auburn hair fanned out against the drab gray blanket, the lights overhead captured the coppery highlights.

He leaned over her, absorbing every detail of her face, from the soft curve of her high cheekbones to the firmness of her jaw. Her face was lightly tanned with a smattering of freckles sprinkled across her nose. She'd always hated that she couldn't go without a hat in the full force of the Texas sun. Her dark red hair and pale complexion made exposure impossible.

Strong, slender fingers, slid across his naked chest, stopping to tweak his nipples.

Adrenaline and something more shot through his body, setting nerve endings on fire. Wade pressed his lips to Lindsay's, savoring the touch, then he shifted to her jaw, teasing a path down the long sleek column of her neck. His hand smoothed over her shoulder and down her arm, rising back up to cup a breast through the ribbed-knit fabric of her shirt.

Lindsay's back arched off the ground, pressing deeper into his palm.

He plucked at the peaked nipple.

She wiggled beneath him, her hands moving down over her belly to the hem of her shirt. She sat up. Pulling the shirt up and over her head, she tossed it onto a bale of hay. Her fingers worked the clasp behind her back and soon her lacy bra followed the shirt.

Full, rounded breasts glowed a peachy cream in the soft lighting, ripe and begging to be tasted.

Wade bent to comply, sucking one luscious nipple into his mouth, rolling the tip across his tongue.

Lindsay grasped the back of his head and held him to her, her head thrown back, her eyes closed.

He eased her to the blanket and laved the other breast until the tip stood taut and puckered. He moved lower, his mouth trailing over her ribs, down to her belly button.

He unbuttoned the rivet on her blue jeans and slid them and her panties down over her legs, his hands following, pressing between her thighs. When he had the jeans down to her ankles, she kicked free of them and the panties, her knees falling wide, her opening moist and tempting beyond redemption.

His body so tight he could explode with need, Wade shimmied out of his jeans and lay between

Lindsay's legs, staring down at her as his erection pressed against her opening. "I've dreamed of this," he said, his voice low and gravelly.

"Me, too." Her hands grasped his buttocks, pressing him closer, but he pulled back, slipping down her body, pressing kisses to her breasts, her belly and the thatch of coppery hair at the apex of her thighs.

He parted her folds and tongued the spot that made her wildly crazy. The place that made her forget everything.

Her bottom rose off the ground and she writhed beneath him.

Wade licked her again, then sucked that little nubbin between his teeth and nibbled. He raised his head, drinking in the vision of her in the throws of passion, her body glowing warm and rosy in the overhead lights.

She cried out, her hands buried in his hair, dragging him back to the task. "Oh, please, don't stop now."

He flicked and teased that special spot, his fingers sliding into her channel, swirling around twisting, again and again.

Her body grew rigid, her breathing all but stopped and she jerked against his mouth.

Wade rose above her, grabbed for his jeans, ripped his wallet from his back pocket and prayed for a condom.

His fingers wrapped around the smooth foil packet and he sighed.

Lindsay took it from him, tore it open with her teeth and rolled the condom down over his rigid member, stroking him along the way.

Beyond patience, way past resistance, Wade slid into her warm, wet opening, burying himself to the hilt, thrusting deep.

She clung to him, her fingers digging into his hips, driving him in and out, faster and harder until the slapping of skin on skin smacked in the silence of the night.

Tension stretched him like a bow string until he couldn't hold back any longer. His release burst from him like a freight train through a tunnel with all the noise, light and commotion of a pyrotechnic show. He held steady for a long, incredible moment, his body pulsing.

Completely spent, he collapsed beside her, rolled her onto her side and spooned her with his body, his hand cupping her breast.

They lay together in silence for several long minutes.

Wade couldn't come up with the words to express what he was feeling. The heat of the moment cooled, leaving him to think too much, to remember all the reasons he shouldn't be lying naked in the barn with Lindsay Kemp.

Nothing had changed, nothing had improved in

his life except the part about having the most incredible sex with the woman he'd never stopped loving.

She deserved a better man than him. Lindsay was the ranch-owner's granddaughter; Wade had always been nothing more than the hired help. Until he landed the job with Bart Bellows, he'd been jobless, homeless and lacked direction in his life.

His hand tightened on Lindsay's breast. God, he wanted her more than anything he'd ever wanted in his entire life. But she'd never forgive him when she discovered his real reason for coming back to the Long K Ranch—to find the evidence to convict her grandfather of attempted murder.

"We need to talk," Lindsay cupped the hand holding her breast.

No, they didn't. He needed to get his head on straight and run this mission like the professional operative he was, not some love-struck teenager.

Wade's hand jerked back and he sat up. What the hell had he just done? Who was he trying to kid? There were more reasons to stay away from Lindsay Kemp than reasons to stay with her. Why couldn't he get that through his thick skull?

"What's wrong?" She turned over and stared up at him, her naked body so tempting that Wade wavered.

No. She deserved better.

"Nothing." He stood, grabbed his jeans and

dragged them on. "You need to get back to the house before your grandfather comes looking for you."

Lindsay's eyes rounded, she drew in a shaky breath. "Are you leaving because I said we need to talk?"

"No." He tossed her clothes at her. "We just shouldn't have done this. It solves nothing."

Chapter Seven

Lindsay pulled her shirt over her head, her cheeks burning, anger and shame making her entire body shake. "What do you mean it doesn't solve anything? What doesn't solve anything? Sex?"

He winced. "I'm sorry, Lindsay. I shouldn't have taken advantage of you. Blame me." He dragged his boots on, hopping away from her as he did.

"Blame you?" She stepped into her jeans, yanking them up her legs, buttoning them with quick, jerky movements. "Who said you were taking advantage of me? Maybe I wanted it as much as you. Did you think of that?" She walked across to where he stood buttoning his jeans.

She pushed his naked chest.

The man made her crazy. When would he learn she wasn't to be toyed with? "All I said was that we needed to talk, and you jump up like your hair's on fire. What is it you're afraid of, Wade Coltrane?" She pushed him again.

This time, he captured her hands against his chest and held them there.

So mad now that she could scream, she tugged to loosen his grip. She wanted to hit him, make him hurt as much as he'd hurt her.

"We don't belong together. We come from two different worlds entirely."

"Haven't you heard? Opposites attract, or don't you get those news flashes from your side of the world?" She stomped on his foot. "Let go of me."

"Not until you calm down."

"I'm calm, damn it. Let go." Her body shook and she feared she'd break down and cry any minute. Damn it, she refused to cry another tear for Wade Coltrane.

That hopeless tear slid down her cheek. "Why do you do this to me?" Her voice caught on a sob.

He stared down at her, his brows dipping low. "Believe me, I never meant to hurt you."

"Then stop doing it." Another tear followed the first.

He pulled her up against him, his lips crushing hers in a soul-shaking kiss.

When he let go, Lindsay staggered backward, her eyes squeezed shut, her hand pressed to her bruised lips. When she dared open her eyes, Wade had gone, leaving the barn door swinging open behind him.

Lindsay swayed, breathing hard, her fingers bunched into tight balls. She turned and slammed her fist into a bale of hay. Straw punctured her skin, making her hand hurt, but not nearly as much as her heart.

She supposed she deserved his anger. Hadn't she pushed him away last time he'd been in town five long years ago? The old adage, what goes around comes around, just came around again.

And she still hadn't told him about the girls.

Rubbing her hand, she left the barn and climbed the hill to the house. Come hell or high water, they had to talk. Whether he wanted *her* or not, the girls were his, and he deserved to know.

Lindsay spent the longest night of her life tossing and turning in her lonely bed, her core aching from the wild sex she'd had in the barn, reminding her of the consequences of sleeping with the aggravating cowboy five years ago. When would she learn to keep passion out of her decisions?

Before the sun pushed over the horizon, Lindsay gave up and climbed out of bed, her eyes gritty, her chest aching and her hand tender and bruised from punching an inert bale of hay.

She had breakfast on the table and the girls fed before the men arrived in the dining room. As soon as boots clunked against wood flooring, Lindsay ducked into her grandfather's office where he sat with the ledger, entering receipts for supplies purchased.

"Your breakfast is ready. If you don't mind watching the girls for a few minutes, I can get started on that cattle chute. Just send them out to the barn when you and the men have finished breakfast. I want to get the chute done before I go to the bank later this afternoon."

"The bank, huh? Tell 'em we just need enough cash to tide us over for a little while. At least until we get the check for the cattle sale." Gramps didn't look up from the heavy ledger, his pencil marking figures in the neat columns, a frown permanently etched in the lines on his forehead.

Now would be a good time to tell her grandfather about what Frank had done in the barn the night before. Her grandfather wouldn't put up with ranch hands manhandling his granddaughter. But the tired, worried expression on his face made her hold back. He had enough to worry about without worrying about her.

They needed cash to keep them going. She'd dipped into the girls' college fund for last week's payroll. She'd wipe out what was left with this week's payroll, especially with the addition of another cowboy to feed and pay.

Lindsay had tried to get Gramps to convert their accounting system to a computer, but he'd refused.

She sighed. "Eat, Gramps, while the food is hot."

"Go on, get out of here, I don't need another woman telling me what to do."

Lindsay smiled at his grumpiness. Deep beneath the gruff surface was a man with a heart the size of Texas. Well, except where the Lockharts were concerned.

While the men consumed the pancakes and sausages she'd arranged on the sideboard, Lindsay left the house to begin work on the rotting boards of the cattle chute. Exhausted from a sleepless night but fired up like a rocket ready to launch, Lindsay had angry, nervous energy to burn off. She hoped it lasted at least until she had the chute repaired.

Even though she still needed to tell Wade about the girls, Lindsay couldn't bring herself to confront him. Not after he'd rejected her the night before. Her ego couldn't handle another irate rebuff from the man. Not so soon after the last.

Lyric and Lacey skipped down from the house less than half an hour later, carrying sugar cubes and apples.

"We brought treats for the horses," Lacey announced, holding out her hands to display her half-melted cube and an apple.

"I'm giving mine to Sweetie Pie." Lyric smiled at Lindsay. "Can I ride her today?"

"Oh, honey, no." Lindsay yanked the top board off one side of the cattle chute. "I have to get the fences around here ready for when the men bring the cattle in."

Lacey's dark brows pressed together, her blue eyes narrowing. "We want to ride."

Lindsay's brows rose. "You know the rules on the ranch. Work comes before play."

Lacey hung her head. "Yes, Mama."

Her daughter looked so dejected that Lindsay

relented. "Maybe we can ride later. Right now, I have too much to do. There is a white bag of screws on the desk in the tack room. Could you get them for me?"

"I'll get them." Lyric ran for the barn.

"No, I will." Lacey raced after her.

"Get the screwdriver, Lacey," Lindsay called out after her daughter. She shook her head and went back to work pulling nails out of the brace posts.

Back in a flash, Lyric had the bag of screws and Lacey carried the screwdriver. They dropped them on the ground where Lindsay indicated and ran off to give their treats to the two horses in the paddock beside the barn.

"Don't go inside the fences and stay away from Thunder. He's been cranky since we took Sweetie Pie out of his pen."

"We will," Lacey called out.

"You will what?" Lindsay jammed some screws into her tool-belt pouch and levered a board up onto the top of the chute. Balancing the board with one hand she used the screwdriver to twist the screw through the board into the brace post.

With each turn of her wrist, she thought of what she'd done in the barn with Wade the night before and her cheeks burned. How would she face him, knowing what they'd shared?

Yet another reason to avoid the man.

What was her hurry to tell Wade about his daughters anyway? She'd already waited five years; what was another two or three days?

Dusty and Billy came down from the house, toothpicks balanced between their lips.

"Mighty fine breakfast, Miss Lindsay," Dusty said. "Thank you kindly."

Billy grunted, gazing at his boots, his cheeks a ruddy red. The man was painfully shy and when he did actually utter words, everyone listened, curious to hear his voice.

"Thanks, guys." Lindsay smiled at the two men who'd been working on the Long K Ranch ever since she could remember. It would be a shame for them to lose their jobs because she couldn't afford to pay them. Payment for the cattle sale wouldn't come soon enough for this week's paycheck. She'd have to ask the bank for a line of credit loan.

Her gaze went beyond the two older cowboys, searching for Wade. "Are you working the north-forty again today?"

Dusty tipped his head once. "Got a couple fences needing repair along the northeast corner.

Good, maybe Wade would go with them.

When Dusty and Billy saddled up and rode out just the two of them, Lindsay's stomach dropped.

Well, drat it all. What was Wade's chore for the day? Lindsay hoped her grandfather didn't get the idea that she needed help with the cattle chute. It was a one-woman job that didn't need a tall, dark and handsome cowboy with commitment issues to help.

Lindsay inserted a screw at the other end of the board, wishing she had a battery-operated screw gun; this chore would go ten times faster if she did.

Once the board was secure, she glanced around. "Lyric? Lacey?" Lindsay peered over the top of the cattle chute.

The girls were nowhere to be seen and it had been a while since they'd checked in.

A high-pitched scream ripped through the air.

Lindsay flew over the top of the cattle chute, dropped to the ground and raced for the other side of the barn.

Boots pounded the ground behind her, but Lindsay didn't take the time to look. Her children were in trouble.

Another scream slashed through Lindsay's heart. Dear God, what was wrong?

When she rounded the corner of the barn her gaze searched feverishly for the twins. A gate hung open to the small corral that housed the Long K Ranch's prized quarter horse stallion, Thunder.

"Get away from her!" Lyric yelled, waving her hands at the stallion.

The black stallion reared, pawing the air with his hooves. He landed close to Lacey who lay cowering on the ground beside his water trough.

Tears and dirt streaked her face, and she clutched her legs close to her chest.

Thunder stood with his back to Lindsay, blocking her path to the girls. He reared and dropped, pounding the earth inches from where Lacey lay on the ground.

Lindsay ran for the open gate.

Before she reached it, hands clamped on her shoulders and shoved her aside.

"Stay back." Wade Coltrane ran into the pen, slowing as he neared the stallion. He spoke in clear, calm tones. "Easy, boy. Easy."

To the girls, he said in the same calm tone. "Be very quiet. Thunder is only scared."

"I'm scared, too," Lacey sobbed from the ground. "I want Mommy."

"Me, too." Lyric's face puckered and she looked across the pen to where Lindsay stood. "Mommy!"

Lindsay held her breath. If Lyric ran, Thunder might spook and trample Lacey. "Stay there, Lyric. Please," she called out.

Thunder snorted, pawing the dust, his hoof dangerously close to Lacey.

Lindsay's breath caught in her throat, and she could barely restrain herself from rushing forward and grabbing the girls from beneath the horse's hooves. Every motherly instinct told her to go, but the rancher in her knew spooking the horse further could lead to an injured child.

"Easy, boy. I'm just here to save you from these

really scary little girls." Wade grinned at the twins reassuringly. To the horse, he spoke quietly, in an even monotone. "It's okay." He circled wide to get in front of the horse where Lacey lay on the ground.

When he was within range, he reached out slowly. "Don't you want to go for a long ride out on the range today, boy? Maybe visit a filly or two? That's right. These silly girls aren't going to hurt you. Come to ol' Wade. I'll take care of you."

Lindsay eased closer, mesmerized by the patience and calm Wade exuded.

Thunder didn't rear, although his hoof still scratched at the ground. He tossed his head toward Lacey, as if admonishing her for having the gall to enter his domain.

Wade reached out to the horse's halter.

The big black stallion flicked his head away and reared.

Lindsay's heart skipped several beats.

Wade stepped between the horse and the girl. If Thunder decided to rear again, his hooves would connect with Wade, not Lacey.

The next time he reached out, Wade caught the halter and immediately backed the horse away from both girls. When he had the beast several yards from the girls, Lindsay swooped in and gathered the girls in her arms.

She lifted them on each hip and ran from the pen.

Once past the gate, she stopped, set them on the

ground and dropped to her knees beside them. "Are you okay? Did he hurt you?"

"I'm okay, Mommy." Lacey's tears had dried, her eyes round. She wasn't looking at her mother, she glanced over her shoulder to the man climbing over the railing of the paddock. When his boots hit the ground, Lacey ran to Wade and wrapped her arms around his legs. Lyric glanced from her mother to Wade as if she wanted permission.

When Lindsay nodded, Lyric shot off to join her sister, wrapping her arms around Wade's other leg.

Lindsay stood slowly, her heart pounding in her chest, the weight of five years of silence bearing down on her shoulders. The girls deserved a father. Wade deserved to know these precious girls were his. She'd had no right to keep the information from him for so long.

Lindsay opened her mouth to tell him.

"Okay, who is going to tell me what happened here?" He dropped to his haunches, his face stern.

"Lyric changed her mind. She wanted to give her sugar to Thunder instead of Sweetie Pie." Lacey let go of Wade's leg, her head drooping.

With a frown pressing down on her forehead, Lindsay closed the distance between her and Wade. "You two know you're not supposed to open the gates."

"We didn't," both girls said in unison.

"Then how did it get open?" Lindsay crossed her arms over her chest, her brows raised.

"It was already open," Lyric said. "Thunder was out here. Lacey tried to get him to come back in. Then he got mad." Her little face puckered and a fat tear rolled down over her cheek.

Wade swung Lyric up and settled her on his shoulders. "And she did a fine job. Only she did such a good job, she scared Thunder."

"No, I didn't." Lacey held her arms up. "Hold me."

"Mr. Wade can't carry both of you on his shoulders at once." Lindsay almost stumbled over the "Mr. Wade" part. What would they call him when they knew he was their father?

Her stomach turned cartwheels at the thought of Lacey and Lyric calling him daddy. When they'd been babies, she'd dreamed of Wade blowing back through town, sweeping her and the babies up in his arms and carrying them off to a happy little picket-fenced house.

After the first year, the dream faded. The reality of raising twins set in as she struggled through late-night feedings and a million diaper changes by herself.

Wade slipped Lyric from his shoulders and into the crook of one arm, lifted Lacey into the other and set them on the rail overlooking Sweetie Pie's pen. "Has your mother taught you to ride?"

"Yes, sir," Lacey said.

Lyric nodded. "We ride Sweetie Pie."

"Did your mother name Sweetie Pie?" He grinned. "I seem to recall pie is her favorite dessert in the whole world."

"It is!" Lacey clapped and almost fell from the top rail. If not for Wade's arm around her middle she'd have fallen the four feet to the ground. "Apple pie."

Lindsay didn't worry. Wade would never let the girls fall and get hurt. He'd always been good with kids, even back in high school. He'd be a great father to Lyric and Lacey.

Again her stomach roiled in anticipation of telling him the big secret.

Not now. Not in front of the girls.

"Come, Lyric, Lacey, you'll have to stay close to me while I finish the cattle chute."

"They can help me clean the tack room, if you can live without them for a few minutes. That's what your grandfather has me doing until he's ready to ride out." He dropped the girls to the ground. "How about it? Think your mama will let you help me?"

Lyric and Lacey rushed to Lindsay, grabbed her hands, shouting, "Please?"

Lindsay squatted down next to them, refusing to lock gazes with Wade, afraid of where her pulse would go if she did. "Are you sure you're all right? Nothing broken, no boo-boos?" She looked to Lacey and then Lyric.

"I'm okay, Mommy." Lacey held up her hands and spun around. "See?"

"Me, too," Lyric repeated Lacey's performance.

Lindsay nodded. "Okay, but—"

All they heard was the okay before they both screamed, "Yay! We get to help Mr. Wade."

"No slackers, girls. You're there to help Mr. Wade." She really had a hard time calling him Mr. Wade, but until she broke the news to him, Lindsay was stuck with the oddity.

"We will." Lyric grabbed one of Wade's hands while Lacey grabbed the other.

The three walked away, the image of the big cowboy and the tiny little girls made a knot the size of a fist lodge in Lindsay's throat. Her eyes blurred and she had to wipe them on the back of her sleeve before she could take a step.

Wade looked natural with the little girls holding his hands.

Tonight. She'd tell him tonight.

First she had an appointment with the loan officer at the bank to request a line of credit loan.

Lindsay completed work on the chute in record time. When she entered the barn to collect the girls, they both looked so disappointed, she almost relented and let them stay. But Wade would be riding out with Gramps as soon as the older man finished with the accounts. That would leave the girls home alone or one of the men would have to stay with them.

"Sorry, girls, you have to come with me." She

herded them to the house where they cleaned their hands and faces and changed into sundresses. Lindsay pulled their long black hair up into ponytails with pretty blue bows to match their eyes.

Determined to make a good impression on the loan officer, Lindsay changed into a slim-fitting dress that complemented the girls' dresses, ran a brush through her auburn hair and dabbed a little color onto her lips. Having taken so long on their appearances, Lindsay rushed out the door, afraid she'd be late for the scheduled meeting.

She couldn't afford to make a bad impression with the loan officer. If she could be late for a meeting, he might assume she'd be late making payments. Lindsay had never missed a payment, and this loan would help her keep her credit record clean. It would also ensure they had the money to pay their workers next week and the week after.

All the way to town, the girls sang songs in the backseat while Lindsay prayed over and over for a change in their luck, a chance to dig out of the slump the ranch had fallen into and couldn't quite seem to climb out of.

At the bank, Lindsay lifted the girls out of the truck and set them on the ground. "You have to be really nice and quiet while I talk about money with Mr. McDaniel in the bank."

Lacey's head tipped to the side. "Is he going to buy the ranch?"

"No, Lacey. We hope he will help us to keep the ranch so that we don't have to sell it."

"Are we going to move to another house?" Lacey asked.

Lindsay gritted her teeth and stared up at the brick-and-glass front of the bank building. "Not if I can help it."

"Our friend, Lucas, moved," Lacey said. "And we won't see him ever again."

"I don't want to move to another house." Lyric's hand slipped into Lindsay's. "I like our house."

"If we move, will Gramps come with us?" Lacey slipped her hand into Lindsay's empty hand and stared up at her.

"We're not moving, sweetheart. We're staying with Gramps."

Lindsay entered the bank, her hands already sweating. She could handle herself with an angry horse, a testy steer or a cranky old cowboy, but dealing with men in business suits always made her nervous.

She paused at a desk inside and asked for Mr. McDaniel.

The woman waved toward a grouping of chairs arranged around an aquarium. "Have a seat over there."

The girls rushed toward the tank, exclaiming over the clown fish and the neon tetras. Lindsay couldn't concentrate, her hearing picking up every sound behind her in anticipation of Mr. McDaniel's arrival.

"Excuse me, Miss Kemp. If you'll come with me, I'll take you to Mr. McDaniel's office." The receptionist led her to a row of glass-walled offices and opened the second door. "Mr. McDaniel, Miss Kemp to see you."

The man left his seat and held out his hand.

Lindsay rubbed her palms down her dress before she took the proffered hand.

"Miss Kemp, please have a seat." He started to close the door when he noticed Lyric and Lacey. His brows rose and he looked to Lindsay. "Yours?"

A flash of anger burst through her. He knew they were hers. Everyone in Freedom knew everybody else. Lindsay clamped down hard on her ire, forcing a smile to her face. "Yes." She took a seat across the desk from Mr. McDaniel and set Lyric and Lacey in the seat beside her.

"I take it you had time to review my loan application?" Nothing like getting to the point, Gramps always said. Lindsay stared straight at the loan officer, her gaze direct, her face schooled into an emotionless mask.

"I did." McDaniel sat in his chair, his elbows on the desk, his fingers forming a steeple. He didn't have the usual stack of loan documents that accompanied a loan.

"Was my paperwork in order?" Lindsay asked, her stomach sinking into her shoes.

"Yes, ma'am, it was." He took a deep breath.

Lindsay's hopes took a nosedive and it was all she could do to sit there and take whatever Mr. McDaniel dished out.

"After careful review of your application and credit scores, I'm afraid we can't extend a line of credit to the Long K Ranch at this time."

"What?" Lindsay leaned forward, her pulse pounding through her temples. "What do you mean you can't?"

"Just that. The underwriters don't think you or your grandfather are good risks. We can't extend a line of credit at this time."

"We have over fifty percent equity in the Long K Ranch. We offered it as collateral."

McDaniel shook his head. "I'm sorry, with the real estate market the way it is, we can't loan based on a dried-up ranch. If we had to foreclose—"

"It's not a dried-up ranch and you won't foreclose because we make our payments."

Mr. McDaniel paused, gave Lindsay a pointed stare and continued. "If we had to foreclose, we'd have no guarantee the ranch would sell in a timely manner. With the market as soft as it is, ranches are more of a liability than an asset. Surely you understand?"

No, she didn't. She didn't understand at all. How was she going to make payroll next week? How were they going to buy groceries for all those hungry men?

"Is that it? That's your final answer?"

He nodded. "I'm afraid so."

Her eyes stung, but Lindsay refused to cry in front of the girls and Mr. McDaniel. She pushed to her feet. "I'm sorry to bother you, Mr. McDaniel. I hope you sleep well tonight."

Her comment was every bit a passive-aggressive jab at the loan officer. Lindsay didn't care. The bank had refused her request for a loan. Not a good risk? They'd never paid a loan payment late, never defaulted on a mortgage. "Come on, girls. Let's go home."

She'd assured them they wouldn't move. At this point, she hoped she hadn't lied to her daughters.

Out on the pavement in the Texas heat, the sun beat down on her. She looked right, then left. What else could she do? Get another job besides the riding lessons? She couldn't make nearly enough money to tide them over until the cattle sale.

Lindsay blamed the bright sunshine for making her eyes water. She just had to hold it together until she got home.

"Can we get ice cream, Mommy?" Lacey asked.

"Not this time, sweetheart. We need to get back and help on the ranch." She didn't add that they couldn't even afford a single ice-cream cone. Every cent counted. Maybe she should collect aluminum cans from the trash containers. Anything to keep from losing the ranch and the only home Lindsay, Lyric and Lacey had ever known.

Lindsay squared her shoulders. Her grandmother had always told her that there was no use borrowing trouble. The Kemps were not moving and they wouldn't lose the ranch…not while she had a breath left in her.

She hurried the girls to the truck, buckling them into booster seats in the back. Riding lessons for the disabled didn't pay much, but at least it was income. It might buy another bag of flour, another can of coffee. If they could limp along until after the cattle auction next week, they might make it—until the next cash flow crunch.

Something had to give and soon.

Lindsay drove the highway home in a daze. She didn't notice the dark sedan in her rearview mirror until the driver gunned the engine and sped up beside her heading into a curve.

Idiot. What did he think he was doing passing on a double yellow?

Lindsay gripped the steering wheel with both hands and slowed to let the other driver go by before someone rounded the bend and slammed head-on into him.

She waved at the driver to go on, but couldn't see through the dark window tint of the sedan.

Instead of passing, the driver slowed with her, remaining abreast in the middle of the curve, in the wrong lane.

Easing as far to the right as she could without

running into the side of a hill, Lindsay increased her speed in an attempt to get ahead of disaster.

The crazy driver beside her kept pace.

With the girls in the backseat of the truck, Lindsay couldn't do what she wanted and flip the driver off. She didn't dare take her hands off the wheel long enough to risk a gesture of any kind. All she could do was slow down and pray.

As she emerged from the bend in the road, she pressed her foot to the brake, the other vehicle increased its speed, slamming into the left front fender of Lindsay's truck.

The girls screamed as the truck wobbled on the road and veered off toward the ditch.

Holding on with all her strength, Lindsay bumped over the shoulder, angled down into the trough and back up onto the road.

The road bent the other way around a large outcropping of boulders.

Lindsay whipped the steering wheel to the left, barely skimming the boulders.

A car raced into the curve from the opposite direction, the sedan veered in front of the truck and slammed on his brakes.

What the hell? Lindsay slammed her foot to her brake. Unable to swerve without hitting the oncoming traffic head-on or the giant boulders on the other side, all she could do was hold on and skid into the back of the sedan.

When the truck collided with the sedan, the sedan lurched forward.

The impact made the truck fishtail and slide sideways in loose gravel. Lindsay held on and prayed she wouldn't hit the other vehicle.

Her hands holding on to the steering wheel with a death grip, she hung on and barreled toward the oncoming vehicle.

The driver swerved slightly at the last moment, barely missing a catastrophic collision with Lindsay's truck.

The sedan driver with the dark tinted windows gunned his engine and raced ahead, leaving Lindsay behind.

A quick glance over her shoulder confirmed her girls were shaken but okay. Closer to home than town, Lindsay continued on to the ranch, her hands clenching on the steering wheel with every car that passed. She'd report the incident to the sheriff when she had the girls safe at home.

What the heck had just happened? Why would anyone purposely try to run her off the road?

Chapter Eight

"What the hell?" Gramps came around his desk and grabbed Lindsay's shoulders. "Are you sure you're okay?" He looked past her to the hallway down which the girls had disappeared as soon as they'd arrived at home. "That lunatic didn't hurt my granddaughters, did he?"

Lindsay hadn't wanted to tell Gramps, but she couldn't get around the dents on the front fender of the truck. He'd find out soon enough and she'd figured she'd get all the bad news out of the way at once.

"And, Gramps?" She sucked in a deep breath and let it out slowly. "The bank refused our loan application."

"Loan be damned!" Gramps thundered. "I'd give them this ranch rather than lose one of my girls any day."

"But, Gramps, after this week, we won't have enough money to pay the men."

"We go to auction next week."

"We won't see that money until the following week and it may not tide us over for long."

"Now don't you go worryin' none. I got things in the works. We're gonna be all right."

Lindsay's brows furrowed. "What things, Gramps?" He'd been secretive lately, sneaking off to go to town in the middle of the day on two occasions Lindsay knew about. He never went to town in the middle of the day unless he had to pick up feed or supplies. Both times he'd come back empty-handed.

Lindsay had chalked it up to coffee drinking with his cronies, but now she wasn't so certain.

"Gramps, I'm just as invested in the well-being of this ranch as you are. I think I should know if you're working on something to do with it."

Gramps shook his head. "No, ma'am. This old ranch ain't gonna support itself much longer, what with big commercial operations taking over the farming and ranching industry. About time I did something to make our lives easier."

Lindsay's breath caught. "You're not selling the ranch, are you?"

The old man looked at her like she was crazy. "No way. I made that mistake once. I refuse to repeat that blunder. No, I just finally got my head on straight. I'm gonna do something I shoulda done a long time ago."

Gramps slipped an arm around her waist and walked her to the door to his office. "Go on, you have a lesson to teach. I'll give the sheriff a call about that car runnin' you off the road."

Lindsay's face flushed with heat. She didn't want to ask but felt compelled to. "Gramps, you aren't doing anything illegal, are you?"

"Go on, get out of here. You'd think I brought you up better than that." He turned, grousing beneath his breath.

Lindsay knew her grandfather lived by the rules. He'd never do anything against the law; it wasn't in his nature.

Her grandfather's assurances did nothing to assuage the heavy load of responsibility sitting squarely on Lindsay's shoulders. She had two little girls to provide for. The ranch was the only home they'd ever known. She'd promised they wouldn't move. But she'd tried everything she knew to fix their financial problems.

Any project her grandfather was working on couldn't possibly conclude in time for them to make payroll. They'd be broke and the money the cattle would bring would barely make a dent in the mounting stack of bills.

As Lindsay trudged out through the back door and down off the porch, she thought back over the time she'd been here on the ranch with her grandfather. Ever since her parents' deaths when she'd only been seven years old, this had been home. Gramps had always taught her right from wrong and that she should always obey the law and be a good citizen.

He wouldn't go against authority to save the ranch, would he?

Not until she reached the barn did Lindsay realize her grandfather hadn't answered her question.

WADE FINISHED work on the fence earlier than he'd expected. He was amazed at how much came back to him after only a few days on the ranch. Old Man Kemp had left earlier to take over the care of the twins while Lindsay taught riding lessons.

As he entered the barnyard, Wade reined in his horse and quietly stared at the corral where Lindsay led a horse around and around in a circle.

The little girl on top had wispy blond hair and a smile as big as Texas on her face. The child's facial distortion indicated the little girl had suffered a birth defect or Down syndrome.

Wade's heart squeezed in his chest. He had a soft spot for the mentally challenged. After his stint in the Army, he'd spent time in rehab with soldiers who'd suffered massive brain injuries. Some would never recover to full functionality. He couldn't imagine what their lives would be like without the love and care of people like the nurses and therapists who'd been there, people with the heart and understanding to work with those who have special needs.

Lindsay smiled up at the little girl, her voice soft and pleasant, her hands gentle with the horse. She was good with her special clients and terrific with her own little girls.

As the lesson came to an end, Lindsay held out her arms for the child to help her down from the horse.

The child slipped out of the saddle into Lindsay's embrace.

Lindsay hugged her tightly, laughing and smiling as she carried her through the gate to the child's mother waiting on the other side.

"Here you go, Brenda. Maribeth is doing wonderfully." She handed Maribeth to her mother.

"I can't get over the difference in her since she started riding lessons." Brenda kissed Maribeth's cheek and balanced her on her hip. "She's like an entirely different little girl. She smiles more, both at home and in public." Brenda hugged Lindsay, tears welling in Brenda's eyes. "You don't know how much that means to me. Thank you."

The touching little scene made Wade want to join the hug fest more than he'd care to admit. He only had to remind himself who he was and why he was at the Long K Ranch.

Hadn't he pushed Lindsay away last night telling her their worlds didn't meet? Wasn't she proving it over and over by the things she did with her riding lessons for the special needs kids? She was the real deal. The kind of person others should be like. Someone with integrity, you could trust and count on.

And Wade Coltrane worked as a spy under her roof, he couldn't be trusted.

Wade dismounted and headed into the barn. He had no business staring at the woman he'd known all along that he couldn't have. Lindsay Kemp deserved more than he had to offer. She deserved a man who could give her everything, a man of honor and courage. Not one who'd break under pressure and place his entire unit at risk. Not a man who could barely pull himself together to complete the job he'd been assigned.

He tied his mount to the inside of his stall, slipped the saddle off the animal's back and hung it on the rack in the tack room.

When he returned with the brush and curry comb, the population of the interior of the barn had increased by one horse and one beautiful woman.

Blood pounded through Wade's veins, shooting his pulse into an erratic rhythm.

Lindsay's back was to him, her hands working at the girth around the mare's belly. Apparently she hadn't seen him enter the barn.

He hesitated, unsure what he wanted to do—retreat to the tack room and avoid her altogether or take over care of her horse and send her up to the house, out of sight and touching distance. He took a step forward, his masculine pride pressing him into action.

Lindsay yanked at the leather strap. "Oh, Sweetie Pie, what am I going to do?"

Wade stopped at Lindsay's quiet entreaty to the horse. He didn't get the indication the girth was her real problem. The tone of her appeal was one of deep and heartfelt desperation.

What did Lindsay have to be worried about? She had a home, her grandfather's love and support and two beautiful girls who also loved her unconditionally.

Lindsay struggled with the leather straps. Her hands trembled and finally smacked the strap and leaned her forehead against the saddle. "Oh, what's the use? I'm out of ideas. I'm tired and I can't fight it anymore. What am I supposed to do? You see how crazy I am? I'm asking advice from a horse." She laughed, the sound choking on a sob. Her shoulders shook and she gripped the saddle so tightly that her fingers turned white.

"What am I supposed to do?"

As she stood with her back to him, quiet sobs ripped a hole in Wade's heart. His feet moved without his conscious thought and before he knew it, he'd come to a stop behind her.

He turned her and opened his arms. Staying away from her wasn't an option. His protective instincts wouldn't allow him to walk away when she was so distressed. "What's wrong?"

She pressed her forehead against his chest, gripping his shirt, her fingers curling into the fabric. "It would be easier to ask what's right." She pulled back, attempting to escape his embrace. "What does it matter anyway? What do you care about me? About the Long K Ranch? About anything other than Wade Coltrane? When have you ever cared? Before long, you'll be out of here. You'll leave. That's what you do best."

Wade still held her in his grip, refusing to let go, no matter how much her words hurt. His lips clamped down hard to keep from telling her everything he had cared about and how it had all fallen apart when he'd been tortured to the breaking point in a terrorist prison camp.

He hadn't come home to a hero's welcome. He had no one to come home to. "You're right, I don't care." The words came out of his mouth, but the actions didn't match. He pulled her to him, his mouth crashing down over hers.

The kiss started as punishment, his lips slanting over her mouth, his tongue thrusting through to conquer hers. His hands slipped down over her shoulders, encircling her waist, wrapping around her like a steel band.

He couldn't have her. Lindsay Kemp wasn't within his reach socially. She could never love a man like him. But he wanted her more than he'd wanted anything and nothing would ever change that. He'd come home five years ago, foolishly thinking he could propose, she'd accept and they'd live happily ever after as man and wife.

It took her sending him away and the harsh reality of a near-death experience as a prisoner of war to hammer it back into him that he could never really have Lindsay Kemp.

But the kiss went on, while, one step at a time, he backed her against the hay.

The barn door swung shut behind him, but he barely recognized the noise, his attention solely on the woman in his arms. When Wade broke off the kiss, he clasped her face between his hands and stared down into her eyes. "I should never have come back."

"When? Now or five years ago?" she asked, her voice a mere whisper, her eyes wide in the dim lighting of the barn's interior.

"Either. I don't belong in your life."

"Then why did you come back?" she asked.

"I was a fool to ever think I could fit in."

"No, you were a fool to leave." She linked her hand behind his neck and pulled his mouth down to hers.

Wade couldn't resist. Once again he let his body make the decisions. He reached for the hem of her shirt and lifted it up over her head, tossing it to the haystack behind her. Then he reached behind her, flicked the clasp on her bra and let the lacy garment slide down her arms.

She stood naked from the waist up, her hair still in the girlish ponytail, but she was anything but a girl. Her body had filled out, her breasts larger than he remembered and she had more curve to her hips.

"Beautiful." He cupped one of the rounded orbs and bent to take a nipple between his teeth, swirling his tongue around the peaked tip and sucking hard.

Lindsay gasped and arched her back, pushing the breast more fully into his mouth.

His arms tightened around her waist and he lifted her.

Her legs wrapped around his waist.

Wade fumbled with the rivet on his jeans. As he flipped it open, a soft pounding sounded behind, jerking him back to his senses.

"Mommy?" A little girl's voice called through the heavy wooden door. "Are you in there?"

Wade dropped Lindsay to the ground. "I'll go see what she wants."

Lindsay scrambled to find her bra and shirt as Wade made his way to the door, buttoning his jeans. What had he been thinking? He couldn't make love to the boss's granddaughter every time he was near her. How would that help him when he had to do what he came there to accomplish? It wouldn't. And she'd hate him even more than she did already.

As he reached for the door to the barn, Wade glanced behind him.

Lindsay had found her bra. She pulled her shirt down over her breasts and sprinted for the exit.

Wade opened the barn door.

Lacey and Lyric, their faces breaking into wide

grins, each grabbed one of his hands and swung off them.

Lacey stopped swinging and looked up at Wade. "We're goin' to the fun-raiser tomorrow, can you come with us? Can you?"

Lindsay's lips pressed into a tight line. "Did you think to ask me first?"

The girls looked to their mother and back to Wade. "Can he, please?"

A sucker for the blue-eyed replicas of their father, Lindsay couldn't say no. She hoped Wade would refuse. "You're welcome to join us, if you can take the time off."

"Mr. Kemp already warned the hands we'd be working half-day tomorrow. We'll be done before it's time to leave for Governor Lockhart's fundraiser."

The girls looked from Wade to Lindsay and back.

Wade grinned and lifted the girls into his arms. "Guess I'm going with you."

"Yay!" the girls yelled in unison.

Lindsay's heart skipped several beats at the picture he made carrying his girls. She made a promise to herself to tell Wade about their relationship. Soon. A breeze lifted her hair, blowing it across her face. She pushed it out of her eyes in time to see horses barreling across the pasture, the riders leaning low over their necks.

The horses' hooves pounded against the dry

Texas ground, stirring up a trail of dust whipped away by the rising wind.

"What the heck?" Wade dropped the girls to the ground, keeping a hand on each until Billy and Dusty pulled their horses to a sliding halt in the barnyard.

"Fire on the range headed this way!" Dusty shouted and swung out of his saddle.

"Where?" Wade demanded.

"Between the herd and here."

Dusty dropped his reins, ran into the barn and emerged carrying burlap sacks over his shoulders and rolling a fifty-five-gallon drum with his foot.

Wade handed the girls off to Lindsay. "Keep them safe. I'll get my truck." He sprinted for the side of the bunkhouse and in seconds had the truck pulled around. The men loaded several fifty-five-gallon drums in the bed and began filling them with water. They tossed shovels, hoes and straw brooms into the back of the truck next to the barrels.

Lindsay, the two girls in tow, hurried toward the house as Stacy Giordano's vehicle pulled into the yard. Lindsay swerved for Stacy's SUV. "Can't do a lesson today. Got a fire out on the range."

"Oh my God." A wide-eyed Stacy climbed down from her SUV. "What can I do to help?"

"If you can get reception on your cell phone, call 9-1-1. Then get Zachary away from the ranch. The men said the fire's headed this way."

"Let me take the girls. I know you'll want to be in the thick of it all."

Lindsay hesitated, staring down at her daughters. Getting them out of the path of the wild fire was the right thing to do, but she just didn't want them out of her sight. Finally, she looked up at her friend. "Are you sure they won't disturb Zachary?"

"Don't worry about him." Stacy smiled over her shoulder at the little boy buckled into the backseat. "We'll manage."

Lindsay smiled her thanks, her heart racing, anxious to get out to the fire and assess the damage. "I'll pick them up as soon as we get the fire under control."

"No hurry. Zachary likes it when they come over to play. And I like having little girls around." She smiled down at the twins. "Lyric, Lacey, wanna come with me to my house?"

"Yes!" the twins shouted in unison.

"Thanks, Stacy."

"Don't worry about it. Take care of the ranch. I'll see you later." She opened the back door to the SUV and the girls scrambled in. "I'll place that 9-1-1 call and then we'll pick up their booster seats on the way out."

Lindsay didn't respond, she was already leaping onto the porch of the house. "Gramps! Gramps!"

Her grandfather met her at the door. "What's wrong?"

"Fire on the range." She executed an about-face, jumped off the porch and sprinted for the truck being prepared for the fight.

Gramps arrived shortly behind her in his beat-up pickup.

The men carried a large plastic water tank from the back of the barn and lifted it into the bed of the pickup. Once they had it secured, Gramps waved them on. "Go! Take the barrels and start to work. We'll come along as soon as the tank's full."

Wade nodded, his gaze going to Lindsay. "Where are the girls?"

Lindsay stood beside Gramps's truck, waiting for the water hoses. "Stacy Giordano is taking them to her place until I can collect them later."

He gathered the water hoses from the barrels in the back of his truck and stuck them down inside the portable water tank. "I guess there's no use telling you to stay here, is there?"

Her jaw hardened. "Wild horses couldn't keep me from coming out to help."

"Then pray for the wind to die down. I'll see you out there." He climbed into his truck, Billy and Dusty leaping into the back with the barrels of water, already dunking the burlap sacks and wrapping them around the straw end of the brooms.

Gramps emerged from the barn with his own stack of burlap sacks. "Don't you worry, Lindsay, girl. We'll get that fire out."

"I just hope no one gets hurt in the process."

Lindsay climbed behind the driver's wheel, her grandfather hauling himself up into the passenger seat.

She hit the clutch, shifted into first and applied gas, following the path left in the prairie grasses by Wade's truck. She hoped the wind didn't shift and sweep the fire straight for the house and barn. But mostly, she prayed that the fire wouldn't hurt the men out there fighting with nothing more than wet burlap.

Lindsay pressed her foot to the accelerator. The old truck shot forward.

Chapter Nine

Wade wiped sweat and soot from his eyes with the back of his sleeve. The heat bore down on him, the breeze a threat rather than a relief. He wanted to shout to the heavens to give them a break, but he didn't, preferring to keep talking to a minimum behind the damp bandana tied over his nose and mouth.

His lungs burned, his eyes stung and his back ached as he dug yet another firebreak in front of the raging grass fire quickly eating its way toward them and the Long K Ranch buildings.

The sun hovered over the horizon, turning the smoke-filled sky a brilliant mauve—what he could see of it through the fog of black billowing clouds rising from the tinder-dry grass.

The county volunteer firefighters had arrived, along with more firefighters from Freedom. Local ranchers and businessmen showed up with bandanas around their faces, carrying shovels and hoes, ready to beat back the fires that could ultimately spread toward their homes and possibly Freedom if the grass fire wasn't controlled soon.

Wade had helped carry Dusty back to the truck when he'd almost been overrun by flames. Dusty had breathed in so much smoke that the paramedic on duty had to give him oxygen.

Flames licked and slapped at the sky, gobbling up dry prairie grass like fuel in a speeding freight train, belching smoke skyward as it raced toward the line of men hurrying to create a firebreak wide enough to halt the fire's eastward progression.

He'd been digging, scraping and turning the grass under for hours now and his shoulders, back and hamstrings ached along with his singed lungs.

He hadn't seen Lindsay's red bandana in more than thirty minutes and he was long past worried. Every instinct inside him begged him to drop his shovel and find her now. For all he knew she could be passed out due to smoke inhalation, lying directly in the path of the fire-spewing monster.

The number of volunteers had swelled to near fifty, all in a line, digging, shoveling, hoeing the ground bare in a twenty-feet-wide swath. If the fire continued in a northeasterly direction, it would run into a creek. Everyone hoped it would do just that. They'd trimmed the branches along the edges of the creek to prevent the fire from hopping over the creek and continuing its destructive path. Now they worked on shoring up the eastern front in case the wind changed directions and sent the flames toward the house. The firefighters hoped to starve the fire of fuel so that it would burn out and leave the rest of the ranch intact.

The firefighter beside Wade looked up, his face pale beneath the black streaks of ash. "Holy crap, the wind switched directions again. Hurry! It's headed this way!"

Wade dug his shovel into the ground, flipped a chunk of dirt and grass upside down so that the grass was buried. He'd been doing this same operation for the past two hours—dig, flip, tamp, move on. His movements had become robotic, his mind drifting on the swirling smoke to one fiery redhead, too stubborn to stay home out of harm's way.

"If you aren't done, leave it!" The firefighter shouted, the roar of the wind and flames upon them. "Run!" He lifted his shovel and ran like a soldier dodging bullets in heavy gunfire.

Wade gripped his shovel and spun in time to see a flash of red.

Not the orange red of flames, but the flash of red was that of the bandana Lindsay wore folded over her face. Several hundred feet to his south, she whacked at the flames inching forward. If she didn't leave soon, she'd be surrounded and unable to escape the grass fire.

"Lindsay!" Wade shouted, his voice carried away by the wind. He switched directions, running parallel to the front of the fire, pushing forward at an alarming rate. "Lindsay!"

Still she didn't hear him, slapping again and again at the fire advancing on her, pushing in on all sides.

When she finally raised her head, the fire had all but ringed her in, smoke climbing higher into the sky as flame consumed fuel in the form of parched grass.

Wade's feet ate the distance between them, his lungs screaming from lack of cool clean air. But nothing would stop him from reaching Lindsay.

Lindsay spun and slapped her burlap sack at the inferno moving in behind her. Over and over she hit the ground until her bag caught fire. She tossed the bag into the blaze, covered her hair and face with her arms and ran through the flames.

When she emerged from the line of smoke and fire, flames licked up the leg of her blue jeans. Instead of dropping and rolling to put the flame out, she ran toward the truck, lighting the grass on fire in her wake.

Wade raced after her. When he caught up, he tackled her, sending her flying into the dirt and tall grasses.

Lindsay lay with the air knocked from her burning lungs, too shocked by the impact to think or move. Hands roughly smacked her legs, then she was flipped onto her back by a man black with soot, a bandana tied around his face, the only recognizable feature the blue of his eyes. "Wade?" She struggled to sit up, but he continued slapping her legs.

"What are you doing?" She looked down as the last spark was extinguished. "Oh my God," she whispered, for the first time aware she'd been on fire. Thank goodness the denim had been too thick for the flames to burn through in such a short amount of time.

"Get up and run, Lindsay." Wade gripped her arms, jerked her to her feet and shoved her toward the trucks fifty yards to the east. "Go!"

"Not without you."

"If you don't go, neither of us will make it."

"Then I'm staying." She stomped at the flames sizzling up the strands of grass. "It has to stop sometime, doesn't it?" She knew grass fires eventually burned out, but when? After it consumed every bit of grass on the ranch? After it overran the house and barn, leaving them homeless?

Lindsay stamped harder on the little shoots of fire springing up everywhere.

Next thing she knew, her world tilted and she'd been swept into strong, muscular arms. Carried away from the flames, she fought against the iron bands clamping her to his chest.

Wade didn't relent, refusing to let her down until they reached the truck.

Behind them, a wall of flame rose higher and higher, whipped by a gust of wind, blotting out the blob of sun dipping below the horizon.

"Good Lord, what next?" Lindsay railed.

"We head back to the house and start preparing for the worst."

"No, we need to stop it here. Now." She kicked her feet, her hands balled into fists, pummeling his chest. "Let me down. Kemps don't quit."

"You can't keep going. You were almost over-run."

"I'd have made it out just fine without your help."

"I know that, Lindsay. You're one of the toughest women I've ever met. But sometimes you have to know when to cry uncle, back up, regroup and come back out fighting."

"I won't let it win. I won't let any of them win." She leaned her cheek against his chest, tears making white tracks through the soot on her blackened face. "I'm just so damn tired of fighting."

"Then just lean back and let me take care of you for a while." He stopped at the truck and slid her into the seat. "Stay here. If the flames get close, get the hell out of here. Got that?"

Lindsay stared past him to the fire burning toward them. "I think we need to leave now."

Wade spun, swore beneath his breath and climbed in beside her, pushing her out of the driver's seat. "Let's get the others."

Driving like his tailpipe was on fire, Wade sped across the grassland, stopping long enough for a man to sling his shovel in the back and jump in the truck bed. The other truck raced toward him, picking up volunteers, firefighters and anyone else unfortunate enough to be fighting a losing battle against wind and fire.

Lindsay stared at flames consuming the Long K Ranch's only source of food for the hundreds of cattle. If they hadn't moved the herd the previous days, they too would have been casualties to the wildfire raging out of control in the summer winds blowing in from the west.

Hunkered down in the seat beside Wade, Lindsay stared out in a daze. Without acres and acres of grass, no matter how sparse, the cattle would have little to keep them fed until they went to market next week. Not that they'd lose a great deal of weight in just one week, but the rest of the herd they'd planned to keep as breeding stock would be hard-pressed to find enough food to hold them over through the majority of the winter.

What little hay they had put aside in the barn wouldn't last long enough to make it to the spring rains.

When they pulled alongside the other truck, Lindsay leaned forward. Billy drove and beside him was one of the local firemen.

"Where's Gramps?" she asked.

Billy looked to the firefighter beside him.

The fireman shook his head. "We thought he was with you."

A giant invisible hand squeezed the air right out of Lindsay's lungs. She yanked the bandana away from her mouth. "Where did you see him last?" She wanted to shout, to rail at Billy for not answering her.

Instead he turned to the volunteer firefighter.

"I saw him about an hour ago around the middle of our firebreak line."

Lindsay clenched her fists to keep from hitting the door. "Go back to the ranch and set up a protective perimeter or whatever it is we need to do to keep the house and barn from burning to the ground." She looked directly at Billy. "Get the horses out of the barn. Move them to the pasture with the big pond."

Billy nodded, whipped the truck around and raced away from them and the encroaching flames.

Wade circled back the way they came.

"I didn't think we missed anyone."

"Standing," Wade added in a low, soft tone. "We didn't miss anyone left standing."

Lindsay's heart tumbled to the pit of her belly.... She prayed Gramps had found another ride back to the ranch house instead of waiting on the rest of them.

They couldn't search long. Anywhere her grandfather might have been would surely have been consumed in flames by now. The men in the back needed to get away from smoke and heat before they became casualties as well. The firefighters had rounded up their men and started moving to a fallback position.

Her gaze panning the ground in front of the advancing fire, Lindsay held her breath, her chest tightening, eyes stinging. They sped down the length of the fire line with no luck, no sighting of her grandfather.

Sick at heart Lindsay laid a hand on Wade's arm. "We have to get the men out of this smoke."

Wade glanced her way, in silent acknowledgment. He spun the truck away from the smoke and flame and raced across the grasslands toward the ranch house, leaving the smoke and haze behind him.

The rooftop of the barn came into view first. Lindsay couldn't believe how close the fire was to the outbuildings. If the wind didn't die down soon, the fire would take everything.

She couldn't tell if the sky was so dark from the smoke or because the sun had finally dropped below the horizon. Either way they had to travel with lights on.

Wade pulled to a stop in the barnyard. The men clambered off the truck, some helping others.

Lindsay pointed to the ones she knew had been at it too long. All of the men were black with soot and ash. Two of them coughed hard, unable to stop. "Jim, Steve, see the EMT. You're out of the fight."

"But, Miss Lindsay—" Steve started and was interrupted with a bout of coughing. When he stopped, he smiled weakly. "Okay, we'll see the EMT. Come on, Jim."

The EMT rescue truck had set up camp in the

middle of the barnyard. A fire pump truck hooked up hoses to the fifty-five-hundred-gallon concrete tank that provided water to the ranch house, the barn and the bunkhouse. Soon they'd spray hundreds of gallons of water on the house and surrounding vegetation to keep it damp when the fire reached the yard.

Lindsay, Billy and Wade moved the horses from the barn to one of the pastures that had been eaten down to the nub in the recent drought. Not much would burn there. If they didn't die of smoke inhalation, the horses might survive.

After they positioned the horses, Lindsay ran to the house, hoping to find her grandfather. She made a quick run through the rooms—no Gramps.

When she emerged onto the back porch, the wind tousled her hair and a line of brilliant red flames pushed toward the ranch.

Why? she wanted to cry out. Why, when they had so many other financial woes, did this have to happen now?

Wade jogged up to the house and slowed when he saw her. "There you are. For a while there, I couldn't find you."

"I can't find Gramps."

Wade climbed the porch and slipped an arm around her shoulders, pulling her close. "He's a tough old bird. He's probably still out there with the firefighting crew, shaking his fist at the wildfire."

A small smile quirked Lindsay's lips and she

managed to chuckle, imagining her grandfather doing just that. "He is stubborn, isn't he?"

"More stubborn than most. Definitely too stubborn to let a fire knock him off his game."

The smile slipped from her lips and tears welled in Lindsay's eyes. "Gramps has always been there for me. I don't know what I'd do without him."

"You have the girls."

"I'm their rock. Gramps is mine." Lindsay leaned into Wade, drawing strength from his solid body; deep inside, she wished she could lean on him always. But their time had come and gone. What they had couldn't be recaptured no matter how much desire remained between them.

When he discovered the truth about the girls he'd likely hate her. And she wouldn't blame him one bit. How selfish of her to keep his daughters from him for all those years.

"Here they come!" Someone shouted from the barnyard.

Trucks loaded with firefighters raced ahead of the raging grass fire, headed straight for the ranch buildings.

"We're going to lose everything, aren't we?" Lindsay whispered. Thoughts of her grandfather foremost in her mind.

"Don't give up yet." Wade's arm tightened around her.

"Kemps never give up, but sometimes it's so hard to keep going when you get beat back so often."

"That's what I love about you. You never stop trying." He bent to press a kiss to her forehead.

It wasn't a passionate kiss, but it was exactly the kind of kiss Lindsay needed at that time. Her arms wrapped around his middle as she stared out at the fire pushed their way by the late-summer winds. She had to get back down to the barnyard and help out, but for the moment, she wanted to soak up the strength of this cowboy to sustain her through the next couple of hours.

"Do you feel that?"

"Feel what?" She lifted her face off his chest. "I don't feel anything."

"Exactly." He smiled down at her. "No wind."

Lindsay lifted her face to the sky. Not a hair stirred on her head. "You're right. Think it's just a lull?"

"No, I think it's stopped for the night."

"Come on! We might have a chance." She grabbed his hand and ran down the porch steps.

Wade liked the feel of her hand in his. Liked that she had leaned on him when she felt all was lost. Liked it a whole lot more than he wanted to. Still he held on and let her lead him down the hill to the barnyard where everyone scrambled, getting ready to go out and attack the grass fire once again.

The trucks filled with the volunteer firefighters that had been barreling toward them a moment before had stopped. The big burly men had unloaded and gotten down to the business of stopping the fire, now that they had a fighting chance.

Dusty met them at the trucks. "Got the barrels and the portable tank full again." When he started to climb into Gramps's pickup, Lindsay stayed him with a hand on his arm.

"You can't go out there again. You've had enough," Lindsay said.

"Got to, Miss Lindsay. It's my life as well as yours. If this ranch fails, I got nowhere else to go." He shook off her hand and climbed into the passenger seat. Billy took the wheel.

Lindsay didn't argue, her heart swelling with pride at the men who'd been with them through good times and bad. She'd do anything to keep the ranch, too. If not for herself, then for her family, both the immediate members or the extended family of the ranch workers who were like uncles to her.

Wade had climbed into his truck and shifted it in gear before Lindsay had a chance to get in. She ran up to the passenger door, grabbed the handle, yanked it open and flung herself inside.

Breathing hard, she righted herself. "Were you going somewhere without me?"

Wade shook his head. "Stubborn, just like your grandfather."

"Damn right." Lindsay stared ahead, searching the line of men silhouetted against the fire. Her grandfather had to be one of them. He didn't give up and he didn't dare die on her. Not yet, not like this.

As soon as the truck stopped, she pushed her bandana up over her mouth and leaped down out of her seat. For the next twenty minutes, she pounded the sparks and embers with wet sacks and her dingo boots.

Without the wind, the fire had nothing to fan the flames. The phalanx of volunteers steadily extinguished the flames until a cheer went up.

Lindsay stomped a glowing ember into the dust and dared to look up. Smoke continued to rise into the night sky, but the raw, red flames had disappeared.

Tears filled her eyes and spilled over, running down her face. They'd done it. They'd saved the barn and ranch house.

Slowly, the men gathered into a group. Lindsay trudged across smoldering stumps of prairie grass and pushed her way through the crowd, staring into blackened faces, searching for Gramps.

At the center of the group, Wade stood, his blue eyes flashing in the starlight, now visible through the dissipating smoke. He had an arm around the middle of a man, holding him up. The man leaned on him heavily, coughing. In between rounds of coughing he grinned, his teeth shining white against his sooty face.

"Gramps?" Lindsay shoved her way past the men

surrounding the older man. "Gramps?" She flung
her arms around the man and hugged him so tightly
that he burst into another coughing fit.

"Lindsay, girl, give a man some air." The old
man's voice was even gruffer than normal, but he
wrapped his free arm around his granddaughter and
squeezed. "We saved her, didn't we?"

"Yes, we did, Gramps." Tears ran freely down
her face.

"What's this?" Gramps reached out and swiped
at a tear.

"I know, I know, Kemps don't cry. Consider it
a first stab at cleaning my face." She smiled, her
heart lighter than it had been in what seemed like
forever. Gramps had made it through. They hadn't
lost their home. The girls were safe in town. Life
couldn't get better.

Lindsay glanced up at Wade. He smiled down at
her, his blue eyes bright spots against his darkened
face. Well, her life could be better, but she'd settle
for having Gramps alive and well and a home to go
to for now.

Chapter Ten

Wade stayed with the volunteers until they were absolutely certain the fire wouldn't flare up again. Lindsay had taken her grandfather back to the ranch house to see an EMT about the amount of smoke the old man had inhaled.

Wade had insisted Lindsay have the EMTs check her out as well.

She'd agreed, but whether she did it was entirely up for debate.

After a shower in the bunkhouse, Wade wandered out into the night, anger keeping him too alert to lay his tired body down and sleep.

The fire chief's preliminary investigation indicated the fire had been a case of arson. An accelerant, most likely gasoline, had been used to get the blaze going. The wind and the dry conditions had done the rest.

When the chief had asked who might have a grudge against the Kemps or the Long K Ranch, one name came immediately to Wade's mind— Frank Dorian.

Wade told the chief of what had occurred in the barn between Frank and Lindsay and Frank's subsequent threat to get even. The chief promised to have the sheriff check into the man's whereabouts earlier that day.

The lingering smoke still infected the country air, but the night was still and the majority of the smoke stayed out to the west.

Stars shone down from the clearing black sky. Wade couldn't begin to count the number of times he'd come out at night as a kid just to stare up at the stars, locate constellations and dream about space travel.

His father had loved showing him the craters on the moon and the rings around Saturn. Wade's mother had given his father a telescope for Christmas one year. He'd cherished that telescope until the day he'd died. Wade still had it, wrapped up in tissue paper in a storage unit outside Ft. Hood. That and the other memorabilia from his past he hadn't had the heart to dig through since his return from the war, from his failure in captivity.

A noise pulled him from his morose thoughts and Wade glanced up at the back porch of the ranch house. A dark silhouette of a person leaned against the porch railing.

After learning of the arson, Wade wasn't leaving anything to chance. He eased his way up the hill, staying low to the ground to blend into the darkness.

He swung wide, to the side of the house. Once he reached the bushes, he clung to the shadows and inched around to the back.

The figure had disappeared from the railing.

Wade's gaze panned the length of the porch, but it wasn't until he came around the edge of the bushes did he find his target sitting on the top step, chin resting in the palms of her hand.

Lindsay sat there in an oversized T-shirt, her legs glowing pale in the moonlight, her bare feet curled over the edge of a step.

"I heard you," she said. "Can't sleep, either?"

Wade chuckled. "I must be losing my touch."

"No, I'm just hypersensitive and too keyed-up to sleep tonight."

"Surprising since you probably inhaled enough smoke to choke an elephant."

She shrugged. "What about you?"

"I'll live."

"Me, too."

Wade dropped to sit on the step beside her.

"I heard the fire chief's preliminary findings." Lindsay stared out at the night. "Think Frank did it?"

"I wouldn't put it past him. He doesn't lose gracefully."

"Part of me wants to take a baseball bat to him."

"You don't know how hard it was not to find the bastard and do just that."

Lindsay nodded. "Then I thought of the example I'd be setting for my girls." She sighed. "As tough as it's been, I need to remind myself of all my blessings."

His arm slipped up her back of its own accord and he pulled her against him. "Top of the list being Lacey and Lyric."

"Right. They had quite the adventure. Stacy brought them home when she knew the fire was out. They're safely tucked in bed, asleep." Her hands slipped around his middle and she leaned into him. "Thanks for being there for us today. You didn't have to fight the fire."

"Yes, I did."

"It's not your ranch."

"It used to be my home. It's yours and those precious little girls of yours." He tipped her face up and stared down into her eyes. "I couldn't let it go down in flames."

"It's the only home we've ever known." Her eyes blinked up at him and she leaned close until her lips were a breath away. "I'd hate to lose it," she whispered.

Wade couldn't resist the invitation. His lips descended to capture hers. He crushed her to him, dragging her across his body until she sat in his lap.

Lindsay's hand circled his neck, pulling him closer still, her tongue darting between his teeth, thrusting against his, swirling and writhing.

Wade's hand pushed up beneath the hem of her jersey night- shirt, reveling at the silky skin of her unfettered breasts. He cupped one, weighing it in his palm, pinching the beaded nipple between his thumb and forefinger.

Her back arched, pressing her breasts against his hand. Her own hand slid down to the hem of his T-shirt and up underneath it. Her slim cool fingers skimmed across his back and around his side to climb up his chest. When she found his nipple, she pinched it between her fingers.

Wade's hands slipped lower to the elastic band of her panties, sliding inside to the mound of hair. He laced his fingers through the curls until he found the folds of skin and the center nub he knew made her crazy. His finger stroked, sliding lower to dip into her juices.

Lindsay moaned, her lips finding his, sealing her mouth over his as she shimmied out of her panties.

His pulse hammering against his eardrums, Wade shifted her body to straddle him, her thighs wrapped around his sides. Nothing stood between them but the denim of his jeans.

Slim fingers reached for the rivet, unclasping it and unzipping the zipper.

Wade let out a groan as his member sprang free into her palm.

She wrapped her hand around him, sliding up to the very tip and back down again.

Wade surged up to meet her. He grabbed her face between his palms and kissed her hard, then transferred his grip to her hips, raising her up over him.

Lindsay bent her knees on either side of his hips and lowered herself down over him, taking his full length inside her, encasing him with her warmth and moisture.

His hands tightened on her hips, lifting up, then letting her settle down over him.

She took control, rising and falling, her pace building with every stroke, faster and faster.

When he could take it no more, he slammed her down hard onto his lap, pressing inside her, holding her steady as he plummeted over the edge of ecstasy. At the last moment, he lifted her up off him, his seed spilling out into air, his erection hard and throbbing.

Even the cool night air couldn't ease the heat that had built inside him. He lay back on the wooden boards of the porch, taking Lindsay with him, tugging her across his chest so that she didn't have to lie against the hard flooring.

She kissed his lips and lay her head against his chest. "Wade, we need to talk."

"Shh." He pressed a finger to her lips. "Talk has only ever gotten us in trouble. Let's just lay here and pretend we don't have a care in the world."

"But we do," Lindsay said, her voice fading into the darkness.

"Not tonight, babe, not tonight."

Too tired to argue, Lindsay let the news she wanted to tell Wade wait until after they'd had a little rest. No use getting all upset when they'd just made love. She'd tell him when they weren't exhausted and they had their heads on straight. Tomorrow.

As she let go of her need to inform him of his daughters, Lindsay allowed herself to revel in his warmth, his hard muscles pressing into her soft flesh. If only they could remain that way forever. If only the world didn't intrude into what they'd just shared.

If only...

She must have drifted to sleep. The next thing she knew, she was being lifted and carried into her bedroom in the ranch house.

Wade laid her down in the sheets, kissed her lips and started to straighten.

"No." She reached up and captured his hand. "Don't go." She was too sleepy to care that she was begging him to stay.

"I can't sleep here. What would your grandfather say?"

She closed her eyes, her hand still holding on to his. "I'm a grown woman."

Wade rubbed his thumb across the inside of her wrist. "To your grandfather, you're still a little girl."

"Please." She tugged harder, patting the bed

beside her with her free hand. "Until I go back to sleep."

"Honey, sleep is the furthest thing from my mind if I lay down next to you."

A smile curled the corners of her lips and Lindsay sat up, winding her arms around his neck. "Same here." She kissed his lips, feathered her fingers through his beard and leaned over to take his earlobe between her teeth. Nibbling softly, she whispered, "Still want to leave?"

"I should." He leaned down over her, pressing her against the pillows, his knees denting the mattress beside her.

"But you won't, will you?"

"Not yet." He lifted the hem of her nightshirt and dragged it up her body and over her head, tossing it to the corner. He stood back and stared down at her. "You're even more beautiful now than you were five years ago."

Lindsay lay naked, basking in the glow of his eyes. Moonlight shown through her window, casting a narrow beam of subdued blue light across his face.

His midnight-black hair glistened in the moon's glow.

Lindsay stretched her arms up over her head, her back arching off the mattress, her knees falling open, inviting.

Wade's chest swelled with the long breath he sucked in. Then he snagged the bottom of his

T-shirt, pulled it up over his head and dropped it to the floor.

His jeans followed and he gently laid his boots on the floor to avoid waking her grandfather.

When he stood naked before her, Lindsay gulped. He was every bit as beautiful as he claimed she was. Even broader and more muscular than the last time she'd seen him naked.

She raised up to touch his chest, trailing her fingers through the fine curls sprinkled across, stalling when she encountered a long scar, buried in the hair. "What's this?"

He stiffened, guiding her hand away from the raised skin. "Nothing."

As soon as he let go, her fingers found the scar again. "It's a big scar to be nothing."

He captured her wrist, squeezing tightly, his jaw hardening. "Leave it, Lindsay."

"Okay, okay." She wrapped her arms around his middle and pressed her lips to his belly. "Leaving it. There are more interesting places to explore." She trailed kisses down his ribs to his belly button, her tongue darting in, then out, sliding lower to the tuft of hair surrounding his stiff erection.

"Much more interesting." She wrapped her palms around his member, guiding it to her lips.

Wade's stiff body grew even stiffer as he waited for her to make the next move.

She took him into her mouth, her lips sliding

down to sheath him until he bumped the back of her throat.

He growled deep in his chest.

The rumble incited fires to flare up inside Lindsay. She clutched his hips, pulling him in and out.

His buttocks clenched and he dug his hands into her hair, pulling her up, off him until she rose up on her knees on the mattress. "You can't begin to realize what you do to me."

"I bet I have a good idea." She leaned into him, the pointed tips of her breasts pressing against his chest, the roughness of the crisp hairs tickling her.

"No." He gripped her arms in a punishing grasp and pushed her away. "You don't."

She stared up into his eyes, recognizing the passion and an even deeper underlying anger. An anger he had no intention of talking about. Unwilling to let him go when they'd only just begun this dangerous dance, she clasped her hands around his waist and refused to be pushed aside. "Show me."

He pressed her back against the mattress, coming down on top of her, his knee nudging her legs apart.

In one fluid motion, he thrust into her, filling her.

"That's a start," she said on a gasp, her body incinerating with the heat of his.

"You ain't seen nothin' yet." He lifted up on his

hands, pushed her wrists above her head, guiding them to the rail of the white wrought iron bed.

Lindsay curled her fingers around the cold bars, eager for this display of animal coupling, eager to let him have his way with her body.

He pulled out and when he drove into her again, her heels dug into the mattress, lifting her hips up to take him more fully.

The rhythm increased, the thrusts coming faster and faster, the springs in the mattress squealing.

Caught on the wave of desire, Lindsay clung to the headboard, her body tensing, her skin and nerves tingling until she catapulted over the precipice, tumbling through a web of sensation until she landed back on earth, her body pressed deeply into the mattress, Wade's crushing the air out of her lungs.

But she didn't care. She wanted him on top of her. Wanted to be dominated and cherished if only for a brief moment. She'd take anything he had to give.

Reality be damned.

She'd face that as the sun came up.

WADE LAY BESIDE Lindsay, her glossy, deep red hair spilling over his shoulder, her breath warming the skin on his chest.

She'd fallen asleep shortly after they'd last made love, exhausted beyond endurance from working as hard as any man, shoveling dirt and slapping wet burlap on the spreading fire. She'd been tough throughout the ordeal, only letting her guard down after the fire was out and everyone was safe.

This was the kind of woman who made a man want to be the best man he could be. She'd always been the center of his universe, the only thing that kept him going throughout his torture in an enemy prison. Even though he'd thought her married to another man, her face, her memory made him want to live in hope of seeing her again someday.

Now he lay with her in his arms, his body satiated, his lust temporarily slaked. But he knew he'd never get enough of Lindsay Kemp. She'd been indelibly etched into his life.

But that nasty monster, guilt, reared its ugly head, making him feel as if he'd played a dirty trick on this wonderful woman. If she had any inkling what he planned to accomplish here at the Long K Ranch, she'd likely shoot him with the gun her grandfather had given her for Christmas her senior year of high school.

As the gray light of predawn edged its way through the window, Wade eased out from beneath Lindsay's sleeping form. Old Man Kemp never slept in. He rose almost before dawn.

Wade wondered if he'd sleep past that time this morning given his efforts fighting the fire the previous night. Either way, Wade wouldn't risk getting caught by the old guy. It would surely destroy his trust and get him fired. Then he'd have failed at his mission. And he couldn't fail. Not again. Failure would never again be an option, no matter how much pain was inflicted on him.

As he slipped off the edge of the mattress, he pulled the sheets up over Lindsay's naked body. She snuggled down, her arm going to the indention his body had left. Her brow furrowed and, for a moment, Wade thought she'd wake.

Then the lines across her forehead faded and a gentle smile curled across her lips.

God, she was beautiful.

Wade gathered his clothing, jamming his legs into his jeans and tugging his shirt over his head. He carried his boots to the door of her bedroom and opened it a crack.

Nothing moved, the place was dead silent.

He tiptoed out into the hallway and out through the back door onto the porch where he sat on the step where he'd made his first mistake the previous evening—slipping his arm around Lindsay.

Wade refused to dwell on the past; he needed to focus on the future and getting the job done so that he could get the hell out of there. Away from the most tempting woman he'd ever known. A woman so far out of his league he couldn't begin to be the man she needed.

If only he hadn't promised the twins that he'd attend the fundraiser with them today, he'd have the opportunity to search Old Man Kemp's office. Everyone planned on going.

Damn, he'd screwed up yet again. He wondered how he could extricate himself out of this situation and not hurt the girls' feelings.

Chapter Eleven

Lindsay stood on the top step of the front porch, wearing her best lemon-yellow sundress with a daisy pattern sprinkled across the cotton fabric. Although the weather was a bit cooler that day, her palms had already begun to sweat and her cheeks burned. The acrid scent of charred grass lingered in the late-morning air, a frightening reminder of what had almost been a devastating tragedy on the Long K Ranch.

Where was Wade?

"Where's Mr. Wade, Mommy?" Lacey echoed Lindsay's thoughts aloud.

"I don't know, sweetie. He might be too busy to come with us to the fundraiser." The logical part of her wanted him to be a no-show. But she held her breath and fought not to fidget like her daughters as they swung on the rails wearing their neatly pressed sundresses, made from the same fabric Lindsay had made hers.

"You girls are visions in yellow this morning." Gramps came out the door, dressed in jeans, a

crisply pressed white dress shirt Lindsay had insisted he wear, with his best rodeo belt buckle pol-
ished and shining at his waist.

Lindsay fussed with his collar. "You sure you'll
be all right attending the fundraiser?"

"What, don't you trust your old grandpa?" He
pecked Lindsay's cheek and patted the twins' heads.
"I wanna be there when she spews her pack of lies.
Gotta know what she's up to. I promise not to do
anything stupid, if that's what you mean."

Lindsay's eyes narrowed. "That covers the doing
part. What about saying anything?"

"You can't take everything a man has from him.
He won't be a man."

Lindsay planted her hands on her hips, her lips
pressing together. "Gramps…"

He clamped his hat on his shock of white hair
and clumped down the steps. "If you ain't ridin'
with me, then leave me be. I have a mind to skip
this shindig altogether and spend my time at the
Talk of the Town sipping coffee."

"You do that, Gramps," Lindsay called after him.
"Might be the best thing that could happen."

"Are you sure you got a ride?" He stared up at
her, shading his eyes from the glare of the sun. "I
could leave the truck and ride in with Billy and
Dusty."

"No, Gramps," she sighed. "We have a ride."

"Yes, we do!" Lacey hopped up and down, a grin

splitting her face practically in two. "We're going with—"

Lindsay jerked Lacey back against her. "A friend. Here, let me fix your bow, it's already falling out of your hair." She leaned over Lacey's perfect bow to avoid eye contact with her grandfather.

"Well, then, I'll be headin' to town," the oldest Kemp said. "Don't let that snake-oil saleswoman con you into buying anything."

"You promised…" Lindsay gave him a warning look.

"I know, I know. You want me to keep my mouth shut. It's mighty hard when all those Lockharts do is spew lies."

"Gramps." She tipped her head downward to the girls who were clinging to every word the adults exchanged.

"What's spew, Gramps?" Lyric asked.

Lindsay's brows rose. "See?"

"I'm gone. See you three later." The old man hurried to his truck, climbed in and spun out of the gravel driveway headed to Freedom.

"Why's Gramps always mad?" Lacey asked.

"I think he likes being cranky," Lindsay responded.

"Anyone ready to go to the fundraiser?" A bright shiny pickup rounded the corner of the house, the deep voice calling out from the window.

Lindsay stared at the truck, avoiding Wade's gaze.

"Looks pretty good for having been through a grass fire."

"Unfortunately it still smells smoky inside. I wiped it down the best I could."

"We appreciate your efforts last night." Her words could have been those spoken to a stranger, stiff, formal, unnatural. Not the words spoken to a man she'd made love to until early this morning. Lindsay risked a glance at Wade's face.

He smiled, his blue eyes tired but bright in the morning light. Wade Coltrane climbed down from the truck and swung Lyric up on one arm and then lifted Lacey on the other. "I believe I have the prettiest girls going to the party with me."

The girls giggled and clung to him as he carried them to the truck.

"I took the liberty of moving the booster seats from your grandfather's truck to mine," he called out over his shoulder. "Nothing but the best for my girls."

Lindsay's head spun, her gaze locking on Wade's back. Had he just said *his* girls? Did he know?

He buckled the twins into their seats and turned to face Lindsay. "What? Is something wrong?"

Everything. "No, nothing." She ducked her head and hurried around to the passenger's side of the pickup.

As she reached for the door handle a large hand beat her to it.

"Now, I wouldn't be much of a gentleman if I didn't open the door for a pretty lady, would I?"

He stood so close that the aftershave he wore curled around Lindsay's senses, reminding her of lying next to him in her bed a few short hours ago. Her body crackled at the remembrance, a fire sizzling low in her gut.

He pulled the door open and waited for her to climb in.

As she stepped up on the sideboard, a hand swatted her fanny.

She squeaked and sat down hard in the seat, her cheeks blazing.

"Ha, ha! Mommy got a spanking!" Lyric cried out.

"No, she didn't," Lacey argued.

"Yes, she did." Lyric's blue-eyed gaze turned dark and stormy. "Didn't you, Mommy?"

"Yes, I did." Her bottom tingled with the lingering warmth of Wade's palm. She fought to sit still, not squirm in her seat, heat pooling low in her belly.

"Did it hurt?" Lacey asked.

"No, sweetie, it didn't."

As Wade took his seat in the truck, he wasn't spared from the four-year-olds' inquisition.

Lyric leaned against the straps of her booster seat. "Why did you spank Mommy, Mr. Wade?"

"It wasn't a spanking," Wade responded. "It was a love tap."

"What is a love tap, Mommy?" Lacey demanded.

Her head began to ache with the responsibility of answering her girls' barrage of questions. "It's when you spank someone but it doesn't hurt."

"Like the time I threw my toys on the floor and you spanked me?" Lacey asked.

"That was different," Lindsay closed her eyes and prayed for a reprieve. "That was a spanking."

"But it didn't hurt." Lacey wasn't giving up.

Lindsay sighed. "It will next time."

"Are we going to eat cotton candy at the fun-raiser?" Lyric asked.

"Maybe a little," Lindsay responded.

A deep chuckle rumbled through the interior of the cab. "Are they always so talkative?"

Lindsay shot a harried look in his direction. "Usually more so."

Wade looked into his rearview mirror. "Did you know that Carrie Rivers will be singing for us today?" he asked the twins.

"Yay!" Both girls clapped their hands.

Lindsay had heard the famous singing sensation would be at the fundraiser.

"I was surprised she was coming to Freedom." Wade maneuvered the truck down the gravel drive and out the ranch gate onto the highway. "It's such a speck on the map for someone that popular."

"My friend Stacy and Governor Lockhart have an inside track with Carrie Rivers. I can't wait to hear her. I have all her music."

"I saw her at a USO show in Iraq. She's very talented."

Lindsay wanted to ask him more about his tour to the Middle East, but didn't dare disturb their tentative truce given his reaction the last time she'd asked. She had so many questions for him concerning his time away from the Long K Ranch. She knew nothing of his life traveling the world. What had happened to him in the Middle East that made him so reserved and angry?

Her chest tightened as she recalled reading report after report in the newspapers and on the online news sources about casualties from the war. She'd prayed again and again that he'd come home safe, even if he didn't come home to her.

Her prayers had been answered. He was safe... physically. But the fun-loving, outgoing young man she'd known in high school had gone. In his place was the serious, bearded man who'd stormed into her life and turned it upside down yet again.

Lindsay stared out the window at the bright sunshine and clear, smoke-free sky. She should be counting her blessings, but instead she was wallowing in morose curiosity, wondering about a man who probably wouldn't stay long. She should sit back and enjoy every minute with him and stop trying to overanalyze every word and action. Live in the moment and forget tomorrow altogether.

Lindsay leaned back in her seat and forced a smile to her lips, determined to have a good day. If not for herself, then for her girls.

A comfortable silence settled over the interior of the truck as the tires ate the distance between the Long K Ranch and Freedom.

As the miles sped by, Lindsay couldn't help but fantasize that this was how it would be if they were a real family. The girls in the backseat, laughing and talking, her and Wade sharing memories and making new ones.

Yeah, and pigs could fly.

Traffic slowed as they neared the small town. Wade turned down a side road and parked along a back street close to the square in downtown Freedom.

WADE DROPPED down out of the pickup and helped Lacey out of her booster seat, and Lindsay unbuckled Lyric. As they walked down the middle of the street toward the center of town, his chest tightened.

Lacey was on one side, her hand in his, Lyric had his other hand and Lindsay walked on the other side of Lyric. To anyone passing by, they looked like a family—father, mother and their twin girls.

Orange traffic cones and wooden barricades blocked the streets from vehicular traffic. They wove their way around them and passed a man

Wade recognized as another Corps Security and Investigations agent. Wade held his breath unnecessarily. The man didn't blink as they strode by, nor did he acknowledge his connection to Wade or Bart Bellow's security and investigations team.

The town square had been cordoned off with a stage erected in the center, draped with red, white and blue banners and placards urging folks to donate to the governor's political party. The local oompah band boomed loud German music from the stage even as roadies set up around them for Carrie Rivers's performance later.

The festive music and the happy faces of the crowd didn't fool Wade. As he panned the streets he discovered a security man on each corner and several lurking around the stage. Beneath the air of celebration lurked a threat. Governor Lockhart had been attacked more than once in the past few weeks. A shindig like this provided a wide scope of possibilities for someone set on ruining her day.

Vendors lined the streets with the traditional Texas fair offerings of turkey legs, funnel cakes and cotton candy. The girls spotted the cotton candy trailer and tugged at Wade's hand, leading him toward it.

Lindsay dug her heels into the pavement. "Not until later. I'd like you two to stay clean and sticky-candy free until just before we leave."

"We'll be careful, won't we, Lyric?" Lacey cried. "Please?"

Lindsay gave them a stern look. "No."

Wade grinned, the little girls' disappointed looks tugging at his heart. "Ah, Mom, it'll wash out."

Lindsay's brows twisted. "You don't fight fair, do you? I promise we'll get cotton candy after Carrie Rivers sings."

"When will she sing, Mommy?" Lacey and Lyric chimed at once.

Lindsay nodded toward the stage. "Looks like she'll be right after the oompah band. They're wrapping up now."

"Yay!" Lacey and Lyric ran toward the band only to be stopped by large hands circling their waists and lifting them high. "You are to stay with me or your mother today. No running off, do you understand?" He purposely made his voice stern, but he softened the warning with a grin.

The girls stared at him, wide-eyed. "Yes, Mr. Wade."

"Besides, you don't want to have to leave early and miss the cotton candy, do you?"

The girls grinned and hugged him around his neck.

A swell of emotion filled Wade's chest. He never would have guessed how good it felt to be adored by two little girls. But it felt damned good. So much so that he wished he could stick around and get to know them even better.

He straightened, reminding himself why he was there. He had a job to complete. A mission that would alienate him to the entire Kemp family, including these precious little girls.

Wade inhaled and let it out slowly. Best to keep on the alert. If someone made a play for the governor, he might not be concerned about collateral damage. Wade would hate to see any one of his girls hurt.

Correction. Lindsay Kemp's girls.

If he'd been as focused on his assignment as he should have been, he'd have bowed out of going to the fundraiser and stuck around the ranch house. While the Long K Ranch workers and family watched the Carrie Rivers concert, he could be searching through Henry Kemp's office and private quarters for the evidence he needed to nail him for the attempts on Governor Lockhart's life.

Then again, if the only reason Henry Kemp came to the fundraiser was to raise more hell with the Lockhart campaign and the governor herself, perhaps he was in the right place.

Wade searched the crowd for Lindsay's grandfather. "Is your grandfather coming to the concert?"

"Against his will." Lindsay smiled across the top of Lacey's head. "He said he'd rather poke a stick in his eye than listen to another one of her campaign speeches, but he had, as he put it, a hankerin' to see Carrie Rivers sing." Lindsay shook her head. "I wish he'd get over his anger and distrust of the governor. She's been nothing but cordial and nice to me ever since I've known her."

A shock of white hair caught Wade's attention.

An older man stood beside a vendor selling barbecue. When the white-haired gentleman presented his profile, Wade could see that it was Henry Kemp, and the vendor he patronized was directly across from the stage where the oompah band was gathering their instruments and hurrying off.

If Henry had a bone to pick with the governor, he'd settled in the perfect position to do just about anything.

Wade hoped the governor's bodyguards were on their toes throughout her speech and as she mingled with the crowd.

Stagehands tested microphones and speaker systems and musicians trickled out on stage, each verifying their electronics one at a time.

Wade's cell phone vibrated in his pocket. As Lindsay explained to the girls what the stagehands were doing, Wade turned away and read the text message displayed. *Hotdog stand, ASAP*. His pulse leaped. The only person who had his cell phone number was Bart Bellows. That he'd risk Wade being seen with him meant he had important news that couldn't wait.

Sliding the phone back in his pocket, Wade smiled at Lindsay. "Anyone want a hotdog?"

"We do! We do!" Both girls hopped up and down.

Lindsay's brows wrinkled, and she shrugged. "I guess it will be all right."

"Tell you what, I'll get them. You stay here with the twins and save our spot."

"Are you sure?" Lindsay looked toward the hotdog stand as more and more people edged toward the stage. "Think you'll make it back before we're sandwiched in?"

"I'll hurry." He went down on his haunches. "Ketchup or mustard?"

Lacey wrinkled her nose. "Just the hotdog."

"Me, too." Lyric added.

"That'll be easy and mess-free. Smart girls. I'll be right back." Wade hurried toward the hotdog stand. Bart Bellows sat in his wheelchair beside the stand, easy to miss in the crush.

Wade ordered the two hotdogs and while he waited for them, he leaned against the side of the stand, close enough to hear what Bart had to say. His gaze panned the crowd for Henry Kemp and he found him chatting with the man serving funnel cakes now. "Aren't you worried this could blow my cover?"

"I had news that couldn't wait," Bart said.

"Shoot."

"As you know, the ballistics on the gun recovered at the Rory Stockett shooting indicated it was a military-issue weapon."

"Yes, sir."

"After checking around at the nearby military posts, we found something."

"Someone reported the missing firearm?"

"Right. A female Spec 4, Adriana Conseco, military police type at Ft. Hood. She got a court-martial out of it. Said that she thinks her ex-boyfriend stole her weapon. She'd brought it to her apartment to show it off, knowing it was against regulations. The weapon should have been locked up in the armory while she was off-duty."

Wade shot a glance down at the wheelchair-bound man. "And do we know who the ex-boyfriend is?"

Bart stared up at Wade, his jaw tight. "Frank Dorian."

Wade swore. "Lindsay Kemp fired him yesterday after he made a play for her."

"Adriana reported they'd broken up nearly three months ago."

"Shortly before Frank hired on at the Long K Ranch." Wade crossed his arms over his chest, he smiled and nodded at Lindsay when she glanced across at him. "Did he give her any clue as to why he might hate the governor?"

Bart shook his head. "None. She did say that they broke up because he was too possessive and more aggressive than she felt comfortable with. He had a hard time taking no for an answer. She also said he seemed to be moody and depressed at times. He didn't tell her what his plans were after their breakup."

"Think Frank's our man and not Henry Kemp?" A spark of hope flared in Wade. He'd like it much better if Frank was their man. As grumpy as Old Man Kemp appeared, Wade didn't want to believe him capable of the attempts on the governor's life.

"Can't say. Henry has motivation. So far we don't know if Frank does, or if he was the one who stole the weapon. Right now it's all hearsay. We're performing a background check on him now, but won't have the results for another day or two."

The man at the hotdog stand held out two hotdogs wrapped in paper. "Here you go, sir. Sorry it took so long."

"Thank you." Wade took the dogs and paid the man. As he turned toward Lindsay, Bart edged out of the gap between vendor trailers and turned his chair in the opposite direction. Then without facing Wade, he gave his orders, "Question Frank if you can. I have to turn the information over to the local sheriff, but if you could get to him first, we might be one step ahead."

"Roger." Wade smiled at Lindsay and wove his way through the masses of people gathering in front of the stage. When he arrived next to Lindsay and the girls, he handed over the hotdogs. "Hotdogs. One for each of you and nothing whatsoever on them."

While the girls unwrapped their treats and tore into them, Wade scanned the crowd. If Frank had a grudge against the governor, he'd be here somewhere possibly ready to take another shot at her.

Nowhere on the square did he see Frank in the

sea of faces. He glanced up at the balconies of the historical buildings surrounding the common area. Men, women and children lined the wrought iron railing, their smiling faces eager for Carrie Rivers to begin singing. A couple of security guards perched on the tops of buildings. No doubt they had rifles at the ready to take anyone out who made a move toward Lila Lockhart.

No sign of Frank.

A movement at the corner, near the bakery caught his attention. Bingo.

Frank Dorian slipped through the throng, a baseball cap pulled down over his sandy brown hair.

Wade recognized him by the way he carried himself. He'd always stood straight, shoulders back, head high, like a soldier.

Wade touched Lindsay's arm. "Do you mind if I disappear for a few minutes before the show starts? I need to see a man about a horse."

"Not at all." Lindsay grinned down at the twins. "The girls and I will be fine. They'll stay busy eating their hotdogs."

His gaze on Frank, Wade took off in the direction of the public restrooms. When he reached the limestone building, he looked back. Lindsay was occupied by the girls. She wouldn't notice if he didn't go right in.

Wade ducked back into the crowd and worked his way toward the bakery, the last place he'd seen Frank Dorian. If Frank had anything to do with the attempts on the governor, Wade wanted to know, even if he had to shake the truth out of the bully.

By the time Wade reached the bakery, Frank had disappeared into the crowd.

Wade had just about given up hope of finding him when he spotted the man emerging from between the barbecue vendor and the funnel cake trailers. He stopped to order something at the barbecue stand and was in the process of paying when Wade caught up to him.

Wade waited until Frank stepped off Main Street and into an alley out of the crush for his chance to corner the guy.

Dorian leaned up against the side of a brick building, his gaze directed toward the stage. He'd just taken a bite of his sandwich when Wade stepped in front of him.

"What do ya want?" Dorian asked around a mouthful of barbecue.

"Where were you yesterday?"

"What does it matter to you? I don't work for the Long K anymore. You saw to that."

"You got yourself fired by messing with the boss's granddaughter. I'd like to know where you were when the grass fire started."

"Don't know what you're talking about."

"I think you started it."

"Got any proof?"

"Not yet, but the fire chief is looking into it. I gave them your name as a potential arson suspect."

"Until you have proof, don't bother me." He lifted his sandwich. "Do you mind? I'm eating lunch."

"One other thing, I learned something interesting."

Frank's eyes narrowed. "So?"

Wade crossed his arms over his chest and studied Frank as he delivered his next words. "Does the name Adriana Conseco ring any bells?"

Dorian's hand with the sandwich paused for a split second on its way to his mouth. "Never heard of her." He took a big bite and chewed.

"That's funny. She seems to know you. Said you were her boyfriend until three months ago. About the time you hired on with the Long K."

Dorian shrugged. "She wishes."

"Did you know she's going before a court-martial for losing a military weapon?"

"Dumb bitch should know better than to bring a military weapon off base."

Wade's brows rose. "Hmm, and you know she brought it off base because?"

"You just said she lost a military weapon."

"Right, but I didn't say where or how."

Frank wadded up his sandwich in the paper wrapping and threw it to the ground at Wade's feet. "If you're accusing me of something else, spit it out or get the hell out of my face."

"Did you hire the shooter that tried to kill Governor Lockhart?"

"If I did, do you think I'd tell you?" Frank stepped

closer to Wade. "You think you know everything about me. Let me tell you what I know about you. You're nothing but a used up ex-soldier who betrayed his country."

Rage erupted inside Wade and he slammed Frank against the brick building behind him. "If I find out you had anything to do with the shooting, or the fire on the ranch, I'll come after you myself, do you hear me? And they won't have to worry about finding the body. There won't be anything left."

"I'm so scared," Frank taunted, though his feet dangled above the ground.

The sound system in the square behind Wade screeched and whined as someone tested a microphone. A voice came through the speakers loud and clear. "Ladies and gentlemen, we'd like to thank you for coming to the fundraiser today. In just a moment, Governor Lockhart would like to thank you herself. Then we'll get on with the Carrie Rivers concert."

A cheer went up from the crowd, but Wade ignored it, his teeth clenched so hard that his jaw hurt.

"You gonna kill me now, in front of witnesses?" Frank clutched at the hands pushing into his throat.

Staring into Frank Dorian's face, all Wade could see were two little girls' bright blue eyes staring back at him accusingly. If he killed Dorian here, he'd be no better than the man and what would the little girls think? They'd be witnesses to his anger and brutality.

The fight went out of Wade and he slowly lowered Frank to the ground.

The shorter man rubbed at the red marks around his neck, a sneer forming on his lip. "You don't have the guts, do you? I know about you. I know you cracked under pressure, that you told the enemy everything about your unit. You're a traitor. A yellow-belly coward."

Wade took a step back, his fists clenched at his sides. "Leave before I finish the job."

"You couldn't. You had no business being in the Special Forces."

Wade slammed the man against the wall again and then shoved him aside.

Frank fell to his knees.

"We aren't through, Dorian."

The man didn't have the chance to spew more venom.

Wade left him on his knees in the alley and circumnavigated the square until he could return to Lindsay and the girls from the direction of the public facilities.

He had to push and press his way through the dense throng until he finally reached Lindsay and the girls.

"I thought we lost you." Lindsay stared at him. "Anything the matter?"

Wade forced his fists to unclench and plastered a smile on his face. "Nothing." *Nothing a well-placed bullet wouldn't cure.*

Chapter Twelve

Lindsay could tell the difference in Wade as soon as he rejoined them. Gone was the smiling man who'd been cordial and patient entertaining the twins.

In his place was a man who was so tense that a muscle twitched in his jaw. She didn't have the opportunity to ask him any more questions because the festivities appeared to be about to begin. But she promised herself she'd get to the bottom of his change in attitude later.

Two burly men carried a podium to center stage. Heavily draped in rich red, white and blue fabric, the wooden stand matched the decoration at the base of the stage.

A technician tested a microphone and finally, a group of muscular men, moved through the crowd. At the center of the group was a diminutive woman in a soft gray skirt suit.

A chill slithered down Lindsay's spine. What was the world coming to when a state governor had to be completely surrounded by bodyguards to go out in public? She clutched the twins closer to her, wondering if she'd done right by bringing them to the fundraiser when the governor had already had a couple attempts made on her life.

Lila Lockhart climbed the steps up to the stage and shooed the bodyguards to the side. With short, neatly styled blond hair, a diamond cross necklace around her neck and a flag pin affixed to her lapel, she looked the part of a diplomat, a politician and a mother all wrapped in one smart package.

Lindsay had read articles about Lila's rise to the governorship and the speculation that she might make a run for the White House in the next presidential election. Not that she'd announced anything, but some predicted this fundraiser would provide the perfect platform by which she could make that momentous revelation.

The media had gotten wind of the speculation and arrived in force for both the governor's speech and the Carrie Rivers concert. They lined the front left corner of the stage, cordoned off by the local police.

The governor nodded toward the podium. "I don't need that. Just the microphone."

The men who'd placed the podium removed it quickly, handing a portable microphone to the governor as they passed behind her.

People gathered around the stage, pressing Lindsay, Wade and the girls in closer. Too close for Lindsay's comfort.

Next to Lindsay, Wade kept looking around over

the tops of people's heads. Wade's constant vigilance made her feel both secure and uneasy at the same time. If he was concerned by all the security, there had to be a problem. Bottom line, she was glad he was there.

Wade wished Lindsay and the girls had stayed home.

After his encounter with Frank, Wade had returned to Lindsay with a really bad feeling about the event. He watched the crowd, looking for anyone acting suspiciously. Frank hadn't moved from the alley where Wade had left him. He stood with his eyes narrowed, a look of pure venom directed at the stage. If looks could kill, Dorian would have slain the politician on stage the moment she'd climbed the steps.

Wade had lost track of Henry Kemp. He panned the growing number of onlookers, but as the crowd thickened, he couldn't isolate the older Kemp's shock of white hair. Nothing. No sign.

The governor's bodyguards moved up alongside the governor, wired for communications with other members of Bart Bellows's security force scattered around the square or strategically placed on the top corners of buildings.

The governor would have none of it. She lifted her hands to the side and physically scooted the bodyguards back. "I'll make this short, 'cause I know y'all didn't come to hear me speak. There's much better entertainment waiting off stage."

The crowd went wild, hooting and hollering for Carrie Rivers.

Lindsay clapped and hugged her girls close to keep them from being crushed between people.

Wade bent to lift them into his arms so that they could hear and see what was going on.

The governor went on, "Thank you all for coming and for all the money we've already raised. Now, I'd like to present our special guest."

A reporter shouted loud enough for most people to hear, "Governor Lockhart, did you have any special announcements to make?"

She tipped her head to the side and gave the man a Mona Lisa smile, secretive and noncommittal. "Now what else would I announce but the tremendous generosity of our special guest for her appearance here in Freedom, Texas? Please give a warm welcome to Miss Carrie Rivers." She backed away as the crowd roared.

The reporters couldn't have asked another question even had the governor been willing to answer.

Carrie Rivers trotted onto the stage, carrying an acoustic guitar and wearing a smile that lit the stage brighter than any man-made lighting.

The singing sensation stopped beside Governor Lockhart and gave her a hug. "Thank you for inviting me to perform in this wonderful town."

She waited for the crowd to settle and continued. "I'd like to dedicate the first song to the men and women of our armed forces who've dedicated their lives to defending our freedom."

As Carrie Rivers's voice lifted and swelled through the amplifiers and speakers positioned at the edges of the stage, the crowd's roar surged to a crescendo and a loud boom shook the ground.

"Get down!" Wade yelled, pushing Lindsay and the girls to a crouching position. People were so tightly packed, they couldn't move, could barely duck.

Bodyguards hustled the governor off the stage into the melee of people screaming and crying. Carrie Rivers stood center stage, her eyes wide, completely frozen. One of the Corps Security and Investigation agents, Vince Russo, leaped up onto the platform, tucked the singer under his arm and ran with her off the stage.

The frightened movement of the masses nearly hid the commotion at ground level by the stage. Then above the rumble of the crowd a woman screamed, "He's bleeding!" The people close to where the governor and her bodyguards stood surged like a ripple in water, pushing outward, away from the nucleus cell of the governor and her protective circle. Women screamed all around them and the horde swarmed outward and away from the stage.

One of the big bodyguards swayed and dropped to his knees, clutching his side. Red stained his white shirt where his hand pressed to his side. His face turned ashen and he fell forward.

Caught in the push, all Wade could do was carry the girls high enough so they weren't crushed, and flow with the tide of humanity pushing to get away from the stage. "Hold on to my shirt and don't let go," he shouted to Lindsay above the noise.

Fingers dug into his sides, wrapping around the fabric of his blue chambray shirt. Lindsay followed him, plastered against his back.

Not until they reached a side street did the throng thin enough that Wade could step to the side and lean against the solid wall of a local business. Lindsay pressed her back to the brick and dragged in deep breaths, one after the other.

"What happened?" she asked.

"I don't know. It sounded like an explosion."

She gasped. "A bomb?"

Wade didn't answer. He handed her the keys to his truck. "Take the girls back to the ranch. I'll find a ride home."

Lindsay shook her head. "I can't. Gramps might still be here. And I can't leave until I know everyone is all right. This is my home. These are my friends."

"I don't like it. What if there's another explosion or stabbing?"

She laid her hand on his arm. "I'll be careful."

"And the girls?" His brows rose. "Are you willing to risk their lives?"

Lyric and Lacey stared up from Lindsay to Wade and back to their mother.

Lindsay chewed her bottom lip for a moment before answering. "I love my girls. I couldn't forgive myself if anything bad happened to them."

"Then get them out of here."

"After I'm sure Gramps and Stacy are okay."

Wade's teeth clenched. "I'll take care of your grandfather. Find Stacy, see that she's okay, and then get the hell out of here."

She raised a hand to his cheek, her forehead wrinkled in concern. "You'll be all right?"

Wade's lips thinned. "I've been through worse."

Lindsay took the keys and her daughters' hands and marched directly for the stage. Right into the path of danger.

Wade might as well have followed her. He couldn't concentrate on anything other than Lindsay and the twins. What kind of private investigator was he if he couldn't stay focused long enough to complete a simple mission?

Wade forced himself to go in search of the source of the explosion, all the while keeping an eye open for Henry Kemp and Frank Dorian. The firefighters who'd set up a fire truck on the square for a demonstration had been first to respond, cordoning off the area around the barbecue vendor's stand.

The vendor lay on the ground, his black and red apron torn and ragged, his face and arms riddled with cuts and bruises. An EMT shone a penlight into his eyes.

"Might have a concussion. Let's get him to the

hospital." They rolled him carefully onto a backboard, applied a stabilizing neck brace and carried him to the waiting ambulance.

The fire chief stood beside the charred remains of a cast iron smoker, its ragged metal edges all the evidence anyone needed to locate ground zero of the explosion. Question was, who set the explosives?

Wade waited until the chief had a spare moment between coordinating the efforts of the first responders and the firefighting team. When the chief had a pause between giving orders and being relayed information, Wade stepped forward. "Any idea as to what caused the explosion?"

The chief shook his head. "No. In most cases of explosions, the explosive material is consumed in the explosion. All the evidence will have to go through the state crime lab before we can pinpoint the materials used."

Wade had two suspects in mind. Henry Kemp and Frank Dorian. Neither of whom were anywhere to be seen. The police had opted to let the people exit the town square rather than retain them for questioning. No one knew if another explosion was set to go off at any moment.

The injured bodyguard had been loaded onto a stretcher and into a waiting ambulance.

Unsuccessful at locating his quarry, Wade joined Lindsay and the girls near the stage where she stood talking to Stacy Giordano, the girls huddling around her legs.

Stacy was shaking her head. "Carrie was so distressed she left in tears."

"I don't blame her." Lindsay hugged Stacy. "I'm glad you and the governor are okay."

"Me, too. Lila was so upset by it all. She blames herself. She's afraid to come out in public again in case *others* are injured by the attempts made on her life."

"How bad was the bodyguard hurt?" Wade asked.

"Stabbed in the midsection. We won't know until they get him to the hospital if any vital organs took a hit." Stacy stared off into the distance, a wan smile curling her lips. "But as bad as it all was, Carrie came through. She insisted on returning to perform for Freedom…*after* the security is tightened and hopefully *after* they find out who was behind the attempts on the governor."

Wade laid his hands on Lindsay's shoulders, his fingers tightening. "Let's get the girls home."

Stacy stared at Wade, then shot a glance at Lindsay, her brows raised.

Lindsay's head shook in a brief negative.

Wade wondered what that was all about but didn't stop to inquire. He lifted the girls up in his arms and led the way to the truck parked safely several blocks away.

While Lindsay buckled Lyric into her booster seat, Wade buckled Lacey. Both girls' heads dipped as they fought sleepiness.

Lacey yawned, her eyelids drooping. "We didn't get cotton candy."

"Maybe next time, sweetheart," Wade promised. Then it hit him that there may be no next time for him. Although Carrie Rivers would be back to perform, Wade might have completed his mission and be gone by then. It wouldn't be him fulfilling that promise to buy the little girls their cotton candy.

His chest ached. He wouldn't be around to rescue them from angry horses, he wouldn't be there to see them off on their first day of school. Hell, what right did he have to even think in that direction?

A few days ago, he hadn't even known of their existence. How could two little girls, barely tall enough to reach his knees, have made such an impression on him? He'd spent the day thinking of them as a family. But they weren't. These girls weren't even his.

He suddenly found himself wishing they were.

The entire time he'd been at the Long K Ranch he hadn't seen Cal Murphy make one move to see Lyric and Lacey. If Wade was their daddy, he'd be there every day to watch them grow and delight in the simple things kids discovered. What kind of father was Murphy to abandon his children?

Wade kissed Lacey on the forehead, shut the back door and rounded to the other side of the truck.

Lindsay shut the back door and reached for the passenger's-side door handle.

"You drive." Wade held out the keys to her.

She stared up at him, her brows drawing together. "Why? It's your truck."

"I want you to drive it home. I have a few things to take care of here in town. I'll find a ride back to the ranch."

"We can wait."

"No, I'd prefer you get the girls home. They look like they could use a nap."

Lindsay snorted. "They'll nap on the way and be primed and ready for anything by the time we get home."

"You're right, but I'd rather know they are safe at home. I want to stay and make sure your grandfather is all right."

"You can probably start at the café. The Talk of the Town will be packed with everyone talking about what happened."

Wade took Lindsay's hand and wrapped her fingers around the keys. "Then I'll start there." This close to her, he could smell the scent of her perfume, a light floral aroma that reminded him of sunshine and wildflowers. Unable to resist, he leaned forward and kissed her full on the lips. He meant it to be a quick, chaste kiss.

Lindsay's hand circled around the back of his neck, and she pulled him closer, opening to the thrust of his tongue. Her breasts pressed against his chest, her warmth and nearness sparking desire low in his belly.

What had started as a kiss, quickly became more until they broke apart, breathing hard.

Twin flags of color flew on Lindsay's cheeks that had little to do with the amount of sun she'd gotten that day. She touched her fingers to her lips and sighed. "I'll see you at the ranch." Then she ducked around him and ran around the truck to the driver's seat.

Wade stepped back and watched as she maneuvered the big truck away from the curb and sped away, glancing back only once.

He shouldn't have kissed her. This whole mission had been a mistake. Every time he went near Lindsay, he made mistakes. But he couldn't find it in his heart to regret even one kiss.

Pulling his head out of a cloud of what must be lust, he set out to find Henry Kemp and Frank Dorian. The sooner he got to the bottom of the attempts on Governor Lockhart, the better off he'd be. He could leave and never look back. Lindsay could go on living her life on the Long K Ranch, raising her children and possibly falling in love.

Wade's fists clenched at the thought of someone else sharing his life with Lindsay. Would he be good to her? Would he treat those two little girls like princesses?

The kicker was why Wade should even care?

He shouldn't.

But he did.

As Wade rounded the street corner and the Talk

of the Town came into view, he spied a white-haired older man entering.

Henry Kemp.

Wade's steps quickened. He had to finish this mission and move on. His sanity depended on it.

People still walked along the street, stopping to talk to each other, their faces worried, their voices low and intense.

A man ahead of him looked familiar from behind. Someone across the street waved and called out, "Dr. Murphy, were you there? Did you see what happened at the square?"

The man in front of him turned, giving Wade a full profile.

Cal Murphy, his rival in high school, gone on to become a pediatrician and the father of Lindsay's two little girls.

Wade's blood boiled. Before he could stop to think through his actions, he caught up with Cal, grabbed his shoulder and spun the doctor around.

Cal's eyes widened and then he laughed shakily. "Oh, it's you, Wade. When did you get back in town?"

"A couple days ago." Wade's fists clenched and unclenched, rage building the more he thought of Lindsay's two little girls, fatherless, the ranch in dire financial straits and the possibility of them all being homeless if things didn't improve. "Why?"

Cal's forehead creased. "Why what?"

Anger pushed him forward and he shoved Cal

in the chest. "What kind of man are you anyway? Why did you abandon them?"

Cal stepped backward, his hands rising defensively. "I have no idea what you're talking about. I haven't abandoned anyone."

All the stress of the day, the explosion, the knifing, the fire the night before…everything…rushed up inside Wade. "You'd deny your own daughters? You're the lowest, most despicable—ah, hell." Wade punched the man in the jaw, sending him flying backward.

Cal landed on his butt on the concrete sidewalk, clutching the side of his face. "Why the hell did you hit me?"

"That was for denying your own children."

"I don't have any children."

"You don't even acknowledge those beautiful little girls? How can you avoid them when they're only as far as the Long K Ranch?" Wade wanted to kick the man into the next county.

Cal's brows rose into the blond hair drooping over his brow and he climbed to his feet, backing out of range of Wade's uppercut. "You think Lindsay's girls are mine?"

"Damn right, I do. You were engaged to marry her the last time I was in town. The timing's right."

Cal shook his head. "Buddy, you got it all wrong. They aren't mine."

"I'm not your buddy." Wade raised his fists but stopped short of swinging again, his hands suspended in midair. Something about the look Cal gave him. The slump of his shoulders didn't look like a man who was lying; he appeared more like one disappointed by the words he spoke. "They aren't your girls?"

"No."

"Then whose are they?"

Cal's lips twisted. "That's not for me to say, even if I knew. You'll have to ask Lindsay. She never told anyone, not even her grandfather. They are the reason we didn't go through with the marriage."

Lyric and Lacey weren't Cal's.

The news hit Wade like a wet blanket, diffusing his anger and muffling his senses. If they weren't Cal's children, who was Lyric and Lacey's father?

Cal's hands dropped to his sides. "You still love her, don't you?"

Wade looked at Cal, not hearing or seeing him, but seeing all the mistakes of his life flashing before his mind. When Cal's question sank in, Wade responded automatically, "Always have."

Cal nodded. "I never could beat you at anything. You were the better football player, you were more popular and you got the hottest chick in the entire high school. What I never understood is why you left Lindsay in the first place."

The reasons had seemed so logical when he'd left, but now, not so much. "I was stupid. I had to prove I wasn't just the foreman's son."

"I get that, but why didn't you stick around when you came back five years ago?"

"She told me to leave."

Cal pressed a hand to his jaw. "I don't think she ever stopped loving you, if that makes a difference. Why don't you stick around this time?"

Wade shook his head. "I won't be here long."

"No?" Cal's hand fell to his side, exposing a bruise already beginning to form on his face. "You'd be making a big mistake leaving that woman. She's one in a million."

Wade couldn't agree more. And she deserved more than Wade had to offer. He nodded at Cal's reddening jaw. "If you're telling the truth and the girls aren't yours, I'm sorry."

"I had a DNA test run. It's official. I'm not their father." He shrugged. "Their real father doesn't know what he's been missing. Remind me I owe you a punch in the face." Cal laughed as he turned to walk away.

Left standing on the sidewalk, Wade felt like he'd been the one punched.

Who the hell was the father of Lindsay's girls?

His stomach roiled, his chest tightening. What man in his right mind could leave them? And how could Lindsay have jumped right out of Wade's and Cal's arms into another man's in such a short time?

His mission forgotten, Wade found Dusty and Billy leaving the café on their way to a poker game out past the Long K Ranch. Wade hitched a ride back with them. They dropped him at the gate and he walked the rest of the way from the gate to the bunkhouse, his brain turning the news over and over.

Cal wasn't the girls' father.

The big question eating away at his insides was who the hell was the father of Lyric and Lacey?

Chapter Thirteen

Gramps entered the house shortly after Lindsay and the girls arrived, claiming he couldn't stomach the hullabaloo everyone was making over Lila Lockhart. He'd left the town square as soon as she started talking, stopped by the Talk of the Town and then headed home. He'd managed to miss all the action.

Lindsay filled him in on the explosion and the stabbing.

Despite his hatred for the Lockharts, Gramps had been concerned over the barbecue vendor whom he'd known since the boy had been in kindergarten.

Still shaken and worried about Wade, Lindsay couldn't stay in the house. After changing the girls and herself out of their sundresses, she paced the front porch until she couldn't stand it anymore.

Gramps agreed to keep an eye on the girls.

Lindsay saddled her mare and rode out to check the extent of damage the grass fire had caused.

After a day of playing "family" she'd come to the decision that no matter what, she'd tell Wade the girls were his tonight. No more stalling, no more excuses. The man deserved to know. And if he chose to be a part of their lives, the girls couldn't ask for a better daddy. Whether they had a future as a family unit wasn't even a question at this point. Lindsay didn't dare entertain that fantasy again.

As she rode out over the charred stubs of grass, Lindsay's heart hurt. On the one hand they'd been fortunate the cattle had been upwind of the fire. But the grass that had burned had been what they were going to graze on until the sale the next week. Now they would have to bring hay out soon, or the herd would be chewing on nubs and losing weight when they needed to be gaining to bring a hefty price.

Why did everything have to be so hard? Why did she have to be so confused? The weight of the ranch, the girls—the truth—weighed on her shoulders so heavily that Lindsay couldn't take it anymore. When her horse plodded to a halt, Lindsay sat staring across the burned pasture, feeling as alone and desolate as the ground she trod on.

She swung her leg over the back of the horse and dropped to the ground, the blackened stubs of grass crunching beneath her feet.

The acrid stench of charred vegetation filled her senses and stung her eyes. Or so she tried to tell herself as tears welled and trickled out of the corners.

They didn't have the money to pay the ranch hands. They didn't even have the money to pay the next mortgage payment. All real problems with no immediate answers. Next week's auction would either make them or break them.

Cattle prices had been all over the board lately, mostly falling. If they had any other choice, they'd wait until prices came back up, but they were up against the wall.

But none of their current financial woes bothered Lindsay as much as the upcoming confrontation she anticipated with Wade.

More tears followed the first.

Wade Coltrane had always been a good man. A man she could trust, a man she could depend on to do the right thing until he'd up and left Freedom to join the Army. Now Lindsay wasn't even sure she knew the new Wade.

And when he found out he was the father of Lyric and Lacey, he'd hate her for keeping the secret from him for all those years. If he was half the man Lindsay thought he was, he'd be livid that he'd missed out on the first four years of their lives.

He'd never forgive Lindsay.

He'd never find it in his heart to love her ever again.

And Lindsay knew that no matter how long he'd been away, how far he'd gone, she still loved Wade Coltrane more than life itself. She'd never stopped loving him.

Lindsay had always prided herself in being strong. She'd had to be as a single mother raising twins.

Now she couldn't seem to stop the sobs rising in her chest. The heaviness of regret pushed her to her knees and she cried.

She didn't hear the sound of horses' hooves until a large gelding slid to a stop, showering her with dust.

Lindsay looked up through watery eyes, the sun blinding her. All she could see was a man on a horse, wearing a cowboy hat, silhouetted against the sky. But she didn't have to see his face to know it was Wade.

She scrubbed the moisture from her cheeks and pushed to her feet, brushing ashes from her hands and jeans.

He didn't say a word as he dropped down out of his saddle to stand in front of her.

The uneasy silence unnerved her. Knowing what she had to tell him, made her hands shake. She sucked in a deep breath and let it out. "We need to talk."

"Yup. I have a few questions."

The blood drained from her head, leaving her feeling weak and dizzy. She forced herself to stand straight. "Questions?"

"I had a conversation with Dr. Murphy."

All of Lindsay's worst fears crashed around her, leaving her breathless and more unprepared for this than she'd ever imagined. She raised her hand. "Please, hear me out. I never meant to keep them from you." More unwelcome tears spilled from her eyes. "I didn't know what to do. I was scared. Oh God, I didn't want you to feel trapped or obligated. I didn't want you to hate me."

Wade gripped her arms and held her up when she would have crumbled to the ground. "What are you talking about?"

As he stared down into her face, Lindsay could tell the exact moment realization dawned.

"Oh God." His fingers tightened painfully on her arms, even as the skin beneath his tan paled. "They're mine."

Wade let go of her and stepped away.

In the late-summer heat, Lindsay's body chilled, a shiver spreading across her skin.

The shock on his face slowly morphed into anger as a ruddy red stain rose up his throat and into his cheeks. "Lyric and Lacey are my daughters."

Lindsay pulled herself together and stood straight. "Yes."

He closed his eyes and inhaled. "I should have seen it."

"They look just like you," she said softly.

His eyes opened, glaring down at her. "Why?"

"I sent you away. I was stupid, confused, engaged to another man and I slept with you."

"And when had you planned to tell me? When they were all grown up?" He advanced on her, grabbed her arms and shook her. "You weren't going to tell me, were you?"

"I never found the right moment," she said weakly.

The words were inadequate even to her own ears. "Keeping them from you was wrong. I know that now. But you were gone to war, several times. I didn't even know how to get hold of you."

"You didn't try." He flung her away from him.

Lindsay staggered backward and steadied. "No, I didn't."

"If I hadn't come back to the Long K Ranch, I'd have never known, would I?"

She nodded, unable to lie to him anymore.

Wade stood there, breathing hard, his jaw clenched tight, not uttering a word, just staring at her as if she was the lowest form of being on the planet.

Lindsay gulped back tears and asked in a tiny, shaking voice, "What are we going to do now?"

Even though they only stood three feet apart, Lindsay sensed a chasm widening between them. She'd never felt this far apart from Wade even when he was at war in the Middle East. Deep in her heart, Lindsay had hoped and dreamed of the day he'd come back to the Long K Ranch and sweep her and the girls up in his arms and carry them away.

That dream lay in the ashes.

Wade Coltrane was a good man, but what Lindsay had done was inexcusable, unforgivable and she'd have to get used to the idea of his hating her.

Wade spun away from her and walked out across the burned wasteland.

Lindsay's gaze followed him, noting the tension

in his broad shoulders, the anger in the placement of each step in the ashes. She couldn't blame him for being mad. She'd have hated him equally if he had kept information about her daughters from her.

Not only had she denied him the knowledge of their existence, but she'd also denied him the joys of watching their first steps, speaking their first words, calling him daddy. The list went on. She'd been so wrong thinking she could live her life as though he'd never existed. Her girls were an everyday reminder that he had a part in their lives.

He strode back across the dull gray grass stubs and mounted his horse without a word. When he finally spoke, his words were short and harsh, "We're not through with this conversation." Wade rode away, leaving a trail of dust and ash for Lindsay to choke on.

She slumped against her horse's neck her eyes dry, her heart empty, unable to shed another tear, wondering if she'd ever learn to breathe again.

WADE DIDN'T SLOW his mount until he came in sight of the herd of cattle, their heads down in their endless pursuit of fodder to feed their bellies. Wouldn't it be wonderful if all you had to do was eat all day long?

You wouldn't have to think or regret what you might have missed.

Lyric and Lacey were his daughters.

He dropped down out of his saddle, his knees nearly buckling as the news hit him all over again. Those two beautiful girls were his. Now he could see it. He didn't know why he hadn't from the very beginning. They looked like him with their black hair and blue eyes.

Geez, he'd been blind.

And Lindsay had stood there right next to them and never said a word.

Damn her to hell!

Wade kicked at the ground, stirring up a fine powder of dust that stung his eyes.

Those precious little girls were his.

As the anger faded, fear crept in with the awareness of the responsibility having children represented.

He'd thought he would complete his mission and get the hell out of Freedom once and for all. He'd never have to see Lindsay again. Never put his heart on the line for a woman he couldn't have.

Now he couldn't escape. Couldn't leave and never look back, unless he left the twins behind. And no matter how bad a father he might be, at least he'd love them and care for them like no one else in the world. They were his flesh and blood.

No matter what Lindsay had done to him personally, Wade couldn't deny that she was a great mother to her daughters. But all children needed a good father.

Wade had lost his mother early in his young life; he couldn't imagine how his life would have turned out without his father as well. Ideally, children needed both a mother and a father to prepare them for the world. Parents who had a loving, solid relationship based on trust and respect.

Not one based on lies. Lindsay had lied to him by omission for almost five years. For that he could never forgive her.

The little niggle of guilt twisted away in Wade's gut. And what had he been doing since he returned to the Long K Ranch?

He'd come under false pretenses, establishing a rapport and working trust with her grandfather, only to enable him to get inside and spy on the old man. In the long run, if what Wade had come to do bore fruit, Henry Kemp would be in jail, the ranch would fail and Lindsay and the girls would be homeless.

How forgiving would she be toward him?

Wade swung up into the saddle and headed back to the bunkhouse. He needed to see Bart Bellows. The situation at the Long K Ranch was more than he could handle. Once again, he'd fail at his mission. But damn it, what could he do? He was damned either way.

He didn't run into Lindsay again, making it back to the ranch where he groomed the horse and then he climbed into his truck. Part of him wanted to stay at the ranch and check on Lyric and Lacey. But he had unfinished business to take care of with Bart before he could begin to think about what he was going to do now that he had daughters to consider.

The truck tires ate the distance to Bart's luxurious mansion on the other side of Freedom. The gates, wired for security, opened as soon as the security guard monitoring the cameras recognized Wade.

Wade sped along the long, curving drive to the big house that perched on a gentle hill in a parklike setting. The grounds, expertly landscaped and maintained, were pleasantly peaceful after the trauma of the burned pastures and the bomb that had just been dropped on him.

His thoughts less than at peace, Wade jumped down from the pickup and took the front steps two at a time.

The door opened before he could knock, a doorman holding it bearing a polite smile. "Mr. Bellows will see you in the study."

Wade nodded and strode toward the bookshelf-lined room. Inside the luxurious office, half the room was taken with the massive mahogany desk behind which Bart Bellows sat in his wheelchair. The lines in his face had deepened since Wade had seen him before the explosion.

"Wade, I'm glad you came." Bart waved toward a chair. "Would you like to sit?"

"I quit," Wade blurted out.

Although his brows rose, Bart didn't display

any other surprise at Wade's blunt announcement. "Please take a seat."

"Mr. Bellows, you won't talk me out of it this time. You don't have to pay me for the few days on the job. I just can't do it anymore."

"I know you weren't happy with the assignment, but could you tell me why the sudden need to abandon your mission?"

The word *abandon* struck Wade right through the heart. His worst fear had come to pass. He'd failed yet again at a job that should have been a piece of cake. "I can't do what has to be done."

"I haven't asked you to do much. Infiltrate and collect, that's all."

"The situation is impossible."

Bart's brows rose up his forehead. "Are you involved with the Kemp woman?"

"Lindsay?" Wade breathed in and out before he answered. "Yes and no."

"That's about as clear as mud." Bart leaned forward in his wheelchair. "I know about your past with Lindsay Kemp. You two were a thing in high school. Is there more than that?"

Wade laughed without a bit of mirth in it. "Yes, sir, more than I'd ever imagined."

Bart sat back and laced his fingers on top of his desk. "Enlighten me, if you will."

He didn't know how to say it other than to be blunt. "The twins are mine."

Bart's bushy gray brows rose higher on his forehead. "No kidding?"

Wade nodded, not yet used to the idea.

"You're a daddy?" A grin split Bart's face and he clapped his hands. "Well, then, that's good news."

"Yes and no."

Bart's grin disappeared. "I take it you didn't know this until recently."

Wade glanced at the grandfather clock against the wall in the study. "I've known for all of thirty minutes to be exact."

Bart whistled. "That could be quite a shock to a man, finding out he's a father."

"She didn't tell me. For all these years, she didn't tell me."

"Quite a blow, is it? Are you finding it hard to forgive her?"

"Forgive?" Wade snorted. "Never."

"Never is a damn long time."

"Not long enough."

"You can wallow in anger," Bart held up a hand to stop Wade from exploding with more words damning Lindsay for her betrayal, "or you can look at the bright side."

"Bright side?"

"When you left Freedom, you didn't have a single relative to your name. Now you're back, and you have two." Bart's grin reappeared. "It's great news. Congratulations, Wade, you're a papa."

Wade stared across at the man, unable to comprehend what the older man was so happy about. Didn't he see? Lindsay had lied to him for almost five years. Then as Bart continued to grin, the other side to that coin flipped in Wade's heart.

He had two beautiful girls. So he'd been robbed of the opportunity of welcoming them into the world. Hell, he'd probably been knee-deep in some operation in Iraq at the time. The Army wouldn't have let him take a break long enough to come home for their births anyway. Still, he'd had the right to know.

He had two baby girls. Twins.

The revelations continued to stagger him and he stumbled toward one of the leather wingback chairs in front of the desk, collapsing before his knees gave out. "I'm a daddy."

"Yes, sir." Bart flipped open a wooden box on his desktop and picked out a cigar, tossing it across the desk at Wade. "Definitely cause to celebrate."

Wade caught the cigar and looked at it without seeing it, seeing instead a hospital with Lindsay lying there, her babies in her arms. How he wished he'd been there. Had he been, he'd have been the proud daddy, passing out cigars to strangers.

But he hadn't been there. Lindsay had delivered twin girls by herself. He couldn't imagine Henry Kemp entering a delivery room. The old man would have been out in the waiting room, pacing and grumbling at anyone who dared to tell him to be quiet.

Lindsay had given birth with no one but the medical staff there to help her along. Wade could imagine how hard it must have been to lie there knowing those two tiny infants were her sole responsibility.

"You don't have to smoke it." Bart's words broke into Wade's thoughts. "I don't smoke them myself. I just roll them around on my fingers. Gave up smoking years ago." He sniffed the cigar and set it back in the wooden case.

Wade stuffed the cigar into his shirt pocket and stood, unsure of his next move, but knowing he couldn't sit still for very long without exploding.

"So what's it to be?" Bart asked. "You want me to replace you, but I can't find anyone who can blend in better than you. You're there, you have a reason to be there. Even more so now that you have daughters to look out for. Do you or don't you want to quit the mission?"

"When Lindsay finds out I'm after her grandfather, she'll never forgive me."

"Do you care? I thought you would never forgive her for keeping news of your daughters from you."

"True, but it's not about us. Somehow she and I have to come to an understanding and soon. I want to be a part of my daughters' lives, but I don't see how it will be possible. If I find evidence to put Lindsay's grandfather in jail, she might do everything in her power to keep me from visiting."

"Tough situation." Bart looked up at him. "Back to my question. Are you staying on or quitting?"

Wade heaved a sigh. "I'm staying on until I figure this thing out."

Chapter Fourteen

Lindsay returned to the house after her horseback ride, mentally drained, her composure so fragile that she'd shatter if anyone looked at her cross-eyed. It was all she could do to remove the saddle from the horse, but she went through the motions of brushing and feeding her mare before turning her out to pasture. She climbed the rise to the house, empty, dragging, wondering where she'd get the energy to go on.

Gramps met her at the back door. "I need to run to town."

Lindsay knew she must look a wreck, but she really didn't care, she needed someone to talk to, someone who would listen without trying to fix things. She needed her friend Stacy. "The girls and I will go with you."

Gramps frowned. "I'll be there on business. Not sure how long it'll take."

"I promised the girls cotton candy. But since the fundraiser ended too soon, maybe they'll settle for apple pie and ice cream at the Talk of the Town."

If Gramps decided to argue more, Lindsay might just break down there in front of him and prove that Kemps did cry after all. Especially when their hearts were breaking into a million pieces.

Her grandfather's eyes narrowed for a moment. Then he turned back into his office. "I'll be ready to go in five minutes. If you're not ready, I leave without you. And do something with your face, it's a mess."

Lindsay barely held it together as she changed from her dirty jeans to clean slacks and a fresh blouse. She rushed through a less-than-adequate repair of her face and ran a brush over her hair.

She counted her blessings that the girls had preferred to play indoors while Lindsay had been out riding. Their clothing remained relatively clean and their hair still bore the pretty yellow ribbons from earlier.

Feeling guilty for dragging them out again after they'd been to town once that day already, Lindsay loaded them into the backseat of the truck, grateful Wade had taken the time to move the booster seats before he'd taken off.

Settled into the passenger seat in just over the five minutes her grandfather had allotted her, she swallowed the sob threatening to rise in her throat. Gramps had little tolerance for tears. He wouldn't understand.

Lindsay gulped, realizing that now that she'd told

Wade he was the father of her children, she had to tell her grandfather. She had no idea how to do it or how he'd react.

As they set the truck into motion, her grandfather cast a glance her way. "You told him, didn't you?"

Lindsay's head whipped around, her pulse leaping into hyperdrive. "What?"

"You told Wade, didn't you?"

"Told him what?" She fought to catch a breath, afraid she'd pass out if she didn't remember how to breathe.

Gramps glanced in the rearview mirror at the little girls in the backseat. "About them."

Lindsay's heart plummeted to her belly. She looked over her shoulder at her two precious girls for whom she'd lay down her life to make happy.

They played with their dolls, unaware of the adult conversation in the front seat.

"What do you know, Gramps?" Lindsay whispered.

"That it was him. I'm not blind, you know, and I can do the math." His mouth twisted. "Hell, I've known all along. I just wondered when you'd get the gumption to tell me."

Lindsay buried her face in her hands. "I'm sorry, Gramps. I've made such a mess of my life."

"You still love him, don't you?"

She lifted her head, her hands falling to her lap.

Misery choked off any words she might have said. She nodded, staring down at her fingers in her lap.

"He drove off like a rabbit with a pack of wolves on his tail. I figured you had to have told him." Her grandfather reached out and patted her arm. "Don't worry, he'll be back. The boy still loves you as much as he did five years ago."

Lindsay shook her head and stared out the side window. "Not anymore. How could he when I kept the truth from him for so long?"

"Love makes fools out of all of us in one way or another. But he'll be back. Mark my words." Gramps gripped the steering wheel and stared straight ahead for the rest of the trip into Freedom. He dropped Lindsay and the girls in front of the Talk of the Town. "I'll be back in an hour." Then he drove off.

Not until he'd left them did it occur to Lindsay to ask him where he planned on going. What business did he have to conduct in town? The bank refused to loan them money. There wasn't another bank in town that would.

Stacy pulled up in her dark SUV and got out. "You told him, didn't you?"

Tears welled in Lindsay's eyes and she couldn't answer without bursting into tears.

"It didn't go well, did it?" Stacy didn't need an answer. She clapped her hands together and squatted beside the girls. "How about a snow cone and a trip to the park to play?"

Both girls jumped up and down, shouting, "Yes, please."

The two women and children walked down Main Street to the snow-cone stand that stayed open during the warmer months. With people still lingering on Main Street, there was a line of children waiting for a cool and colorful treat.

Lyric picked her favorite blue-coconut flavor and Lacey chose the cherry. Once they had their snow cones dripping down over their hands, the four girls walked to the park and found a shady table to sit at.

Lindsay and Stacy chatted about nothing until the girls had consumed as much of the snow cone as they were going to finish and tossed the rest. After a quick rinse under the water fountain, Lyric and Lacey ran off to play on the swing set.

An awkward silence followed. Now that she was away from the ranch and she'd had time to calm, Lindsay felt bad about dragging her friend away from her job. "I'm sorry, I shouldn't have called. Governor Lockhart—"

"Will survive without me for a couple of hours." Stacy put an arm around Lindsay's shoulders. "Besides, she was so traumatized by everything that after the police cleared out, she laid down with orders not to be disturbed until tomorrow. I was on my own except for a few phone calls."

"Thanks for coming. I didn't know what to do."

"Tell me what happened." Stacy listened as Lindsay spilled the story.

Lindsay made it all the way through without shedding another tear, her eyes dry, her heart sore. She gazed out across the park at her girls, laughing and playing, completely unaware of the momentousness of the day. They had a father.

"Well, the good thing is that the girls will now know who their father is." Stacy must have been a mind reader in her past life. "When are you going to tell them?"

Lindsay sighed. "I don't know. I think Wade has the right to choose how and when."

Stacy nodded. "That's only fair. My bet is that they'll be over the moon. I saw how good he was with them at the fundraiser before all hell broke loose."

Lindsay's lips lifted slightly. "He will be a good father."

"Any chance he'll take on the role of husband, too?"

Lindsay shook her head. "I don't think he'll ever forgive me. Heck, I wouldn't forgive me if I were him." She sighed again. She seemed to be sighing a lot lately.

"You'd be surprised what relationships can weather. And those little girls would be worth the effort of mending the rift between you two adults."

Lindsay closed her eyes. "I wouldn't want him as a husband if he only did it for the girls."

"No? From what I can tell, you love the guy, right?" Stacy crossed her arms over her chest.

"Yes." Lindsay swallowed hard to keep from sobbing.

"I'd think you'd take him any way you could get him. The rest will fall into place when you two get over yourselves and remember that you love each other."

"But he doesn't love me."

"Oh, baby. Yes, he does." Stacy smiled and patted Lindsay's hand. "It is as plain as the nose on your face. The man is besotted. He's just a little mad right now. He'll come to his senses."

"I don't think so."

"Wanna put a little wager behind that?" Stacy stuck her hand out. "I bet you Wade Coltrane will come to his senses within a month, probably less."

Lindsay avoided the outstretched hand, her eyes narrowing. "I didn't think you were a gambler."

Stacy laughed. "What do you think campaign managing is but a big high-stakes game of cards?"

A smile quirked the edges of Lindsay's lips and then fell. "I don't have any money to bet with."

"Heard anything from the bank?"

"They turned down my loan application."

"Well, darn." Stacy sat up straight and looked

across at Lindsay cheerfully. "I know, I have a couple thousand in my savings account. I'll happily loan it to you."

Lindsay held up her hands. "No, I can't take money from friends. It would ruin the relationship we have. And that I won't allow. I need you in my life."

"Same here. The offer stands, though. Just say the word and the money is yours." Stacy hugged her close. "Your grandfather will be back to pick you up soon at the café. We'd better get there or he'll be grousing at me for holding you up."

"His bark is worse than his bite."

"I know, but I'd just as soon not test it, either. I've already had a heck of a day." Stacy ran a hand through her hair and sighed. "I'm ready to call it done."

"Me, too. And I'm beginning to think it isn't over yet."

"You've already told Wade the news, what's the worst that can happen now?"

"Don't ask, it might jinx me." Lindsay knocked her knuckles on the wooden picnic tabletop for luck, tension building in her stomach at the possibilities of all that could go wrong with the rest of what was left of a disastrous day. Hell, a disastrous week.

WADE HAD DRIVEN around town for several minutes looking for any sign of Frank Dorian or his truck. He had questions for the man, but the jerk wasn't to be found.

It didn't make sense for Frank to target the governor. What motivation did the man have to want to cause Lila Lockhart harm? Despite the lack of motivation, Wade didn't trust the man. Who knows, maybe Frank had a thing about authority figures? Enough so that he'd want to target the governor. Deep down, Wade hoped it was Frank and not Henry who'd set off the explosion and stabbed the bodyguard.

Wade had spotted Lindsay, Stacy and the twins walking down Main Street carrying snow cones. His heart swelled up into his throat. Those girls were his. Sweet Jesus.

He almost stomped on the brakes and jumped from the truck, but he didn't know what he'd say to Lindsay or the girls. He hadn't thought that far ahead.

What would he say to Lyric and Lacey? Had Lindsay already told them? Would she leave it to him? How did you tell four-year-old girls that you were their daddy?

Oh, but he wanted them to know. The thought of those sweet little girls looking up at him and calling him daddy made him want to shout.

Instead he turned down a side street and left town, convinced he wasn't ready. Not yet. Not when their great grandfather might be involved in attempted murder and Wade Coltrane was on the case to expose the man.

He arrived at the Long K Ranch intent on cornering Henry Kemp and asking him what he knew about the explosion and the stabbing in the square earlier that day.

He parked his truck in front of the bunkhouse and made a quick pass through the bunkhouse and barn. No one was there.

He marched up to the house determined to have it out with Henry. The truck wasn't there, but it wouldn't be if Lindsay had used it to take the girls back to town.

Wade rapped sharply on the solid wood back door.

No one answered, but the door was unlocked as was the habit of many who lived so far out.

He twisted the handle and entered. Maybe Henry hadn't heard his knock. "Henry?"

No answer. The house, usually filled with the cheerful sound of little girls' laughter, stood as silent as a tomb.

If he ever hoped to find evidence of any foul play on Henry's part, now would be the perfect opportunity. He had the house to himself. Hopefully the ranch hands wouldn't return anytime soon.

Wade started at the back of the house, heading for Henry's bedroom first. He searched in the closets, under the bed, in shoeboxes and old suitcases. Nothing. No knife, horseshoe nails, nothing.

He worked his way through the hall closets and into the girls' room. Not that he expected to find a murder weapon among dolls and dresses.

As he stood in Lyric and Lacey's room, a huge knot lodged in his throat. Twin beds covered in pink-and-white quilts sat on either side of a window. A dollhouse stood in the corner next to a tiny table and chair set. Teddy bears and dolls sat in the chairs around the table as though they'd come for a visit and tea.

It hit Wade in the gut. What did he know about little girls? What kind of father would he be to Lyric and Lacey? He couldn't teach them how to do their hair or which pretty outfits they should wear. Suddenly overwhelmed at his inadequacy, he backed out of the room and closed the door.

All he knew were horses and football. Then he remembered Lacey and Lyric wanting to ride the other day. He could ride with them.

Depending on the outcome of this investigation. If he found anything on Henry Kemp, that would be the end of his welcome on the Long K Ranch. All his visits with the girls would be at his house, not at the ranch. He didn't have horses; he barely had a backyard.

Wade saved Henry Kemp's study for last. It had a French door out onto the porch he could use if he needed to get out fast.

Quickly, skimming the bookshelves, he zeroed in on the old wooden desk that had been in the Kemp family since Wade could remember. His father had helped with the books when he'd been alive. Wade had been in and out of that office so many times during summer vacation that he'd felt at home in the Kemp household.

Thus the wad of guilt growing like a sponge in his belly. He sat in the cracked leather chair and methodically searched each drawer, working from the top downward.

When he pulled out the bottom left drawer, the floor dropped out of Wade's world. There in the back he found horseshoe nails and a knife with dried blood on it.

Sweet Jesus. It was the evidence needed to nail the man behind the attempts on the governor's life.

For a long moment, Wade stared at the nails and the knife without touching, without moving.

What he had to do next would seal his fate with Henry and Lindsay Kemp. Neither would ever forgive him for his actions.

Knowing he had no choice, he lifted the phone from its receiver and dialed Bart Bellows's direct number.

"Bellows." Bart answered after the first ring.

"I found it," Wade said, his voice flat and disembodied.

"What and where?"

"Horseshoe nails like those used on Governor Lockhart's road and the knife used in today's stabbing. Here at the Long K Ranch in Henry Kemp's desk."

A long pause followed Wade's announcement. "I'll call the sheriff. Stay with the evidence until he arrives."

"Yes, sir."

"And Wade?" Bart paused.

"Sir?"

"I'm sorry."

"Me, too." Wade replaced the phone on the desk and looked up at a sound in front of him.

Lindsay Kemp stood framed in the doorway, her face pale, her eyes glazed. "What have you done?"

He answered with a question, "What did you hear?"

"Horseshoe nails and a knife?" She entered the room and circled the desk to stare down into the drawer still open. She gasped. "Oh my God. Did you put those there? Did you plant those in my grandfather's desk? Are you setting him up to take the fall for you?" Her pale face reddened and before Wade could react, her hand snaked out and slapped him hard across the cheek.

She backed away, her eyes wide, staring at him.

Wade slowly stood, anger rising at her accusation. "I didn't plant the evidence. It was there."

"My grandfather wouldn't have done those things. He's grumpy but he's a good man."

"Anger has a way of making good people lose sight of what is good and bad."

"Not Gramps."

"The evidence is damning, Lindsay." Wade glanced down at the knife. "If that knife is found to be the one used to stab the bodyguard today, there's not much anyone can do to protect your grandfather."

"But he didn't do it." Lindsay shook her head from side to side, then she stopped and looked up at Wade, her eyes narrowing. "What were you doing in here anyway?"

Heat rose in Wade's cheeks, a burning path of guilt. "I was looking for evidence."

"Evidence?" She closed her eyes, biting down hard on her bottom lip. "What are you, the police?"

Confession time had come and it wasn't any easier than Wade had anticipated. "I'm a private investigator. I was sent here to investigate your grandfather."

"In which case, you lied to me." Lindsay reared back to slap Wade again.

This time he caught her wrist before her palm could connect with his face. "I did my job. I hired on with the Long K Ranch to get close to Henry Kemp. It's what I do. Infiltrate the enemy and discover their secrets."

"And use those around them to gain access, don't you?" Lindsay jerked her hand free. "You used me to get to my grandfather. Was everything we did a lie?"

"No. Lindsay—" He reached out to take her hand, but she backed away.

"Don't touch me," she said, her voice catching on a sob. "Don't ever touch me again."

"You weren't supposed to be here," Wade felt like a wide chasm had opened up between him and Lindsay, too wide to cross. "You were supposed to be married. I didn't plan on hurting you."

"You've hurt me by hurting someone I love."

"And you didn't hurt me?" Wade threw back at her.

"I thought you were at war. I was pregnant, confused and thought I was in love with you. All these years, I thought I loved you." Lindsay laughed, her voice catching on the tears welling in her throat. "I didn't even know who you were."

Sirens sounded in the distance.

The front screen door opened and closed with a slam. "Lindsay? Are you all right in here?" Henry Kemp called out. "I hear sirens. What's happening?"

Lindsay's gaze captured Wade's, tears welling in her eyes. "You tell him."

"Mommy?" One of the twins cried out. "I'm scared."

Lindsay turned toward the door and called out, "We're in the study."

Henry Kemp entered first, the twins crowding

through as they spotted their mother. Lyric ran for Lindsay. Lacey ran to Wade and grabbed his hand, leaning against his leg.

"What's going on here?" Henry asked. "What's happened?"

Lindsay took Lyric and Lacey by the hand and led them out of the room. As she passed her grandfather, she leaned close and hugged him. "I know you're innocent. I love you."

"I want to stay with Mr. Wade," Lacey said, looking over her shoulder.

"Not now. We need to get baths and get you two ready for bed." Lindsay said, her voice too tight and strained to be normal.

Wade's heart ached as his daughters and the only woman he'd ever loved disappeared down the hallway. He took a deep breath and let it out. He faced Henry Kemp, fighting to mask his emotions and finish the job he'd come to do.

Chapter Fifteen

Lindsay went through the motions, settling the girls in the tub. Once she had them playing with toys and unaware of what was about to go down, Lindsay slipped out into the living room.

The sheriff had cuffs on her grandfather's wrists.

The old man wasn't talking. He stared at Lindsay, every line in his weathered face more pronounced, aging him more than his years. "I'll be all right, Lindsay, girl. You stay here. I don't want the twins to see all this. It might scare them."

Lindsay hugged him, unable to talk past the lump in her throat. Tears spilled down her cheeks.

Gramps shook his head. "Remember, Kemps don't cry."

She shook her head. "Yes, they do, Gramps. Yes, they do."

Wade was outside in the yard, his hands hanging at his sides, his face an impassive mask.

Lindsay stared at him, wondering who he was.

Had she ever really known him? She ducked back inside to check on the girls.

They were happily playing with their tub toys, splashing each other and getting the bathroom floor soaked. Lindsay didn't let them see her wet cheeks.

By the time she ran back to the front of the house, the sheriff was helping her grandfather into the backseat of his SUV and was shutting the door. Wade had disappeared.

Lindsay felt like she'd had her heart cut out of her chest. She stood, torn between racing out to beat on the sheriff's car for taking her grandfather and checking on her girls. Lindsay stood for a moment longer, watching as the vehicles pulled away leaving the yard empty. Once the taillights disappeared in a cloud of dust, the only sound remaining was that of the cicadas stirring to life as the sun set over the Long K Ranch.

After another peek at the girls, Lindsay ran for the phone and called the only friend she had. Stacy.

Lindsay hated relying so heavily on her, but she had no other choice. She couldn't abandon her grandfather to the legal system.

Her grandfather had let them take him without a fight. What was wrong with the cantankerous old coot? He never went down without a fight.

When Stacy answered, Lindsay blurted out the whole mess, ending on a shaky plea, "Please, help me."

"Good grief. And I thought my life was on edge."

Stacy agreed to get a sitter for Zach and come to the house and stay with the girls while Lindsay visited her grandfather at the jailhouse.

By the time Stacy arrived, Lindsay had the girls in their pajamas, packed an overnight kit for her grandfather, arranged for her grandfather's attorney, Gordon Smith, to meet her, and she'd bitten off three nails.

"I don't know how long I'll be," Lindsay kissed the girls on the forehead. "Be good for Miss Stacy and don't get too rambunctious, please."

"We'll be good, Mommy," Lyric said, combing her doll's hair.

"What is rambunctious?" Lacey asked.

Stacy laughed. "Don't worry about us. We'll be fine."

Lindsay ran for the truck, slid in and cranked the engine.

She could see the bunkhouse through her windshield, but there was no sign of Wade's truck. He'd done his job, he wasn't obligated to stay, nor was he welcome.

Lindsay drove into Freedom, her head spinning with all that had happened in the past twenty-four hours. She thought of her grandfather sitting in a cold, impersonal cell, away from the comfort of his home and bed. She thought of her girls and how they'd grow up without a male in their lives with their grandfather in jail and their father...well.

He certainly wouldn't be welcome on the Long K Ranch after this.

She pictured the look on Wade's face when he'd shown her the knife and nails. He didn't look like a man who'd hit the jackpot. He hadn't smiled or said "Aha!" He'd had a pained expression, like a man facing a firing squad.

Lindsay shook those thoughts from her mind.

Wade Coltrane had tricked her and her grandfather. He'd come to work at the Long K Ranch undercover to nail her grandfather for something he didn't do.

Lindsay could see how they'd suspect Henry Kemp of wanting to hurt the governor. He'd loudly proclaimed his desire for revenge on more than one occasion in public. But if anyone knew Henry Kemp like Lindsay did, they'd know he was all wind and that he wasn't capable of hurting someone in that way. He wouldn't have hired a gunman to take a shot at Lila Lockhart, and he wouldn't have stabbed the bodyguard.

Would he?

Then again, he'd been acting suspicious lately. Like where had he gone by himself today? What "business" had he conducted?

Lindsay stomped her foot on the brake as she pulled into the jailhouse parking lot. She refused to even consider her grandfather responsible for any wrongdoing where the governor was concerned. He was a grump, not a killer.

Which brought her back to one big question. If Wade hadn't planted the evidence in her grandfather's drawer, who had? Who would be that malicious? Who had the opportunity between the stabbing in the square and Wade finding it in the drawer?

Lindsay entered the jailhouse to find Gordon Smith had arrived and was in a conference room with the sheriff and her grandfather. A deputy checked her identification, even though he knew her, then led her back to the room. She didn't know what she'd be able to do to help her grandfather, but someone had to be his advocate. As his only adult relative, the job was hers.

As SOON AS the sheriff had taken charge of the evidence and Henry Kemp, Wade had gone to the bunkhouse, packed his belongings and left. He figured Lindsay wouldn't want him to stick around, not after having her grandfather arrested for attempted murder.

He knew he was delaying the inevitable. They would have to come to some arrangement concerning visitation. Unless Wade signed over sole custody to Lindsay. Life would be easier for her if he did.

Besides, what kind of daddy would he be to those beautiful, trusting little girls? He'd proven he couldn't stand up under pressure when he had given over information about his unit. He'd proven he couldn't be trusted. Lindsay could attest to that.

Hadn't he come to the ranch, taken advantage of Henry's confidence and trust in him, only to betray the man by turning him in?

Maybe the twins would be better off without a father who had such a pitiful batting average.

He couldn't even take pride in a mission accomplished. Despite all his training as a Special Forces soldier, Wade Coltrane had come to the conclusion that he wasn't cut out to do this kind of work.

On the highway, Wade steered his truck toward Bart Bellows's mansion to hand in his resignation. Perhaps he could find work as a janitor or in a factory counting widgets.

The gate swung open when Wade neared, as though Bart had been expecting him.

Parking in the circular drive, Wade dropped down from the truck and climbed the steps to the front door. The door swung open and Bart himself waved him inside.

"Come in, come in. I have news for you."

"I'm not coming in." Wade stood on the porch, refusing to enter. "I quit."

Bart heaved a big sigh and stared up at Wade. Finally, he said, "I won't accept your resignation unless you come in and listen to me first." He backed his wheelchair into the foyer and waited for Wade to cross the threshold.

Every fiber of Wade's being told him to turn and walk away. But he couldn't. Call it a sense of duty or respect for the man who'd seen in him someone worthy of a second chance, Wade couldn't walk away without giving Bart the last word.

He stepped through the door.

Bart led the way to his study and rolled in behind his desk. He clicked his computer mouse, the flash of the screen lighting his face. "I found out some interesting facts about Frank Dorian."

"What's the use?" Wade turned toward the window overlooking the manicured gardens. He didn't see the beauty of the flowers or the last of the sunshine as evening set in; all he could see was the disappointment in Lindsay's eyes. "The evidence we needed was in Henry Kemp's desk."

"Cleverly placed, don't you think?"

Wade turned, his eyes narrowing. "What do you mean? You think someone planted the evidence?"

"I told you I found some interesting information on Frank Dorian. Come see."

Wade's pulse quickened and he rounded the desk to look over Bart's shoulder at the computer screen.

"I did a little background check on Frank and discovered his real name is Francisco Dorian."

"So?"

"Check out this article from *Austin Chronicle* about a Mario Dorian."

Bart wheeled back to give Wade access to read the article.

Mario Dorian had been involved in selling drugs since he was fifteen. At twenty, he'd raped and murdered a young woman. When he bragged to one of his gang members about his conquest, the gang member's girlfriend had notified the police and Mario was arrested. The evidence had been irrefutable, the jury trial short. Mario Dorian had been found guilty and sentenced to death.

His mother, Maria Dorian, had appealed to Governor Lockhart last year to stay his sentence and spare her son's life. The governor had refused and Mario Dorian was put to death by electric chair.

"I take it Mario and Frank are related?" Wade asked.

Bart reached across and clicked the mouse, bringing up an article from a small-town newspaper in south Texas. The clip was about the suicide death of one Maria Dorian dated a few days following the execution date of Mario Dorian.

Bart clicked again and an obituary for Maria Dorian filled the screen. He read aloud, "Survived by her son Francisco Dorian."

"His motivation." Wade straightened, his heart racing, his fists clenching. "It was Frank, not Henry Kemp."

"And I'd bet my last dollar Frank planted the evidence in Henry Kemp's desk because Henry was so vocal about his hatred of the Lockharts."

"And Frank was fired by Henry. Our man Frank likes revenge. Which means I sent the wrong man to jail and a potential killer is still out there." Wade was already on his way to the door before he finished the sentence.

"I notified the governor's bodyguards to be on the lookout for Frank Dorian. I also left a message for the sheriff. He was in a meeting. We believe the knife Dorian used is one he stole from his ex-girlfriend. Once we get her to identify the knife, it'll clear Mr. Kemp. He'll be home to sleep in his own bed."

"In the meantime, Lindsay and the girls are alone at the ranch. If he's into revenge… Damn." Wade burst into the open, leaping to the bottom of the steps.

Frank Dorian's ex-girlfriend had said he was extremely possessive and aggressive. After his misfire-knifing attempt on the governor today, he wouldn't be stupid enough to go up against heightened security around her home.

Given Frank's propensity toward anger and violent behavior, he might be looking for payback on his other recent failure.

Lindsay Kemp's rejection.

Wade jumped into his truck, cranked the engine and ripped out of the circular drive hitting fifty by the time he reached the conveniently opened gate to the Bellows estate.

He could be chasing air, but rather chase it than risk Lindsay and his daughters' lives.

LINDSAY ARRIVED home after only an hour in the sheriff's office, listening to the sheriff's charges and the attorney's rebuttal. When all was said and done, her grandfather remained in his cell and she could do nothing until the district judge set bail.

Like they had any money to post bail.

She hated leaving her grandfather there, knowing he preferred the comfort of his own bed and pillow, but what else could she do? Stacy couldn't stay all night, and the girls needed their mother as much as she needed them.

Sad, hurt and drained, Lindsay arrived home and sat behind the wheel for several seconds before she could bring herself to move. When she finally got up the nerve to go into the house, she climbed out of the vehicle and ascended the steps by the light of the fingernail moon.

It wasn't until she raised her hand to the doorknob that she noticed that all the lights were out in the house.

Her pulse spiked. Maybe the electricity had gone off. Stacy wouldn't turn out all the lights. If the girls woke in the night to complete darkness, they freaked.

Lindsay twisted the knob, but the door was already open and swung inward. Alarm bells went off in her head.

"Stacy?" she called out, flipping the switch for the hallway light.

Nothing. No light, no sound.

Adrenaline jumped in her veins and she shot

down the darkened hallway to the girls' room. "Lyric? Lacey?"

She burst through the closed door and ground to a halt.

Silhouetted in the starlight shining in from the windows stood a man dressed in black with a black ski mask covering his face. "Do anything stupid and I'll break their necks."

In each arm he had a twin, duct tape covering their mouths.

They squirmed, tears coursing down their cheeks.

Lindsay froze, blood pounding hard against her eardrums. "Don't hurt them," she begged. "Do what you want with me, but don't hurt them."

"Now that's more like it. Not so uppity when given a little motivation, are we?"

Lindsay knew that voice, had heard it in a darkened barn recently. "Frank?"

He chuckled, the sound sending chills across Lindsay's skin. "Took you long enough."

"Let the girls go. It's me you want."

"Yeah, but these brats are my key to you."

"I swear I'll do anything you want, just let them go."

"Tempting, but I don't trust you." He motioned her toward the door. "Let's take this little party outside."

Lindsay nodded. "Okay." She backed through the doorway and into the hall.

"Not so fast. Stay where I can see you or one of your brats gets it."

"I'm here. I'm here." She stopped and waited for Frank to close the distance. The girls whimpered, their feet flailing to the sides. Rage burned deep in Lindsay's chest, but she couldn't act on it, not when her daughters needed her to keep a cool head. Her heart broke at every tear, every whimper, but she couldn't show weakness. "It's okay, sweeties. Everything is going to be fine."

"Move." Frank kicked out at Lindsay, landing a heavy boot to her shin.

She winced, biting down hard to keep from yelling in pain. The girls would be even more frightened than they already were.

As she moved through the house, she wondered where Stacy was and whether she'd been hurt or… gulp…

No, she refused to believe her friend had been killed by this monster.

Pounding sounded from inside the girls' closet, making Lindsay's head jerk around.

"Damn woman. Guess I didn't hit her hard enough."

Lindsay let go of the breath she'd been holding. Stacy was alive. Thank God. Now to get her girls away from this madman before he hurt either of them.

Her mind worked furiously as she moved down the long hallway toward the living room. How could she get him to let go of the girls without hurting one of them?

When she reached the living room, Lindsay paused. "Where to?" The delay gave her time to study the area around her. She couldn't hit him. Her swing would only give him time to twist and she might hit one of the girls. She had to surprise him so that he threw his hands in the air, letting the girls loose. She had to trip him backward and fast or he'd take the girls down with him.

"We're going to take your truck and get the heck out of here," Frank said.

Directly in front of Frank was the rug the girls liked to use sliding down the hall on the wooden floors. It was slippery and Lindsay invariably had to pull it up to keep anyone else from falling on it. If Frank was to step on it...

"Leave the girls, take me." Lindsay backed up another step.

Frank stepped forward, one foot on the corner of the slippery rug. It didn't slip. "I'm taking all of you."

How could she get him to slip on the rug when he held her girls? "Your hands are full. How will you manage?"

"Don't you worry about how I'll manage. I've got ways."

Starlight shone through the window, glancing off the knife he held against Lacey's belly.

All the air left Lindsay's lungs. It was one thing

to trip him if he only had hold of the girls, but a knife made it an entirely different game.

"Why are you doing this?"

"Let's just say I'm tired of you rich bitches thinking you can control everyone's lives." He spat on the floor. "You're no better than that killer governor. She didn't see fit to let my brother live. He was only a kid, not much older than these brats." He shook Lyric and Lacey.

The girls whimpered, their eyes begging her to help them.

Lindsay was helpless in the face of this threat. "What does the governor have to do with you wanting to hurt my children?"

Frank went on as though he didn't hear Lindsay's question. "My mother, God rest her soul, was the only decent woman in this stinking world. Lila Lockhart signed her death warrant when she denied my brother's stay of execution. She killed both my brother and my mother when she refused to stop it." The rage and torture in Frank's voice bordered on maniacal and frightened Lindsay to her very soul.

"I'm sorry about your mother, Frank. I'm sorry your brother died. But two innocent children's lives won't bring them back." Lindsay backed up another step and dropped to her knees. "Please, please, let my children go." She bowed as if in despair, her fingers bunching on the other end of the rug.

"Get up, fool!" Frank kicked out at her.

Lindsay jerked her head back, but his boot caught her temple.

Pain shot through her head as she yanked with all her might, praying her girls would be all right.

Frank Dorian's feet flew out from under him. His hands flailed to the side, the girls falling free of his grip.

"Run!" Lindsay screamed at Lyric and Lacey. "Run outside!" She grabbed the rug and pitched it over Frank's face.

Lyric and Lacey rolled to the side and jumped to their feet. Lyric ran for the back door. Lacey followed. Their bare feet pattering against the wood flooring.

Lindsay leaped to her feet and dived for the lamp beside her grandfather's easy chair. She yanked the cord from the wall and turned toward Frank.

He'd come to his knees, tossing aside the rug, his eyes bulging, his lips pulled back in a snarl. "You're dead."

Lindsay's blood ran cold. She lifted the heavy ceramic lamp and aimed it at Frank's head.

As she slammed it down, his hand came up, catching it in mid-swing.

He twisted his hand and sent the lamp crashing against the wall. Then he reached out and clamped his meaty hand around Lindsay's wrist. "Now we do things my way."

Chapter Sixteen

Wade pulled into the yard at fifty miles per hour, slamming his foot on the brakes to skid to a halt in a cloud of dust. He slung the door open, but before his boots touched the ground, he heard the screams of little girls. Adrenaline punched through his veins and he leaped toward the sound he guessed to be out behind the house.

From around the side of the house, Lyric and Lacey burst into the light of the sliver of a moon. They slid to a stop when they saw Wade headed their way and screamed again.

"It's me, Mr. Wade," he called out.

About to run the other direction, the two girls turned as one and raced toward him, sobbing.

He dropped to one knee and opened his arms.

The twins flung themselves at him, crying and babbling so fast he couldn't begin to understand a single word.

Then Lyric gulped in air and grabbed Wade's cheeks between her little hands. "That bad man is going to hurt Mommy."

Wade gripped each child's shoulder and he stared into faces wet with tears. "Where is your mommy?"

"In the living room," Lacey said, hiccupping.

His hand tightened on their shoulders. "Girls, it's very important that you do what I say," he said quickly. "Run as fast as you can to the barn and hide in the hayloft. Don't come out until your mother or I comes to get you. Don't come out for anyone else, do you understand? No matter what they might say. Promise?"

"We promise." Lacey sniffed and reached for Lyric's hand.

"Now run." He turned them around and gave them a pat to send them on their way. He watched for only a moment as they ran around the side of the house.

A CRASH INSIDE the house made his heart flip and he raced toward the front door. He took the porch steps two at a time and as quietly as he could. Rather than rush in, he peered through the window into the living room.

The darkness inside made it difficult to make out shapes. But then a large figure loomed over a smaller one and the flash of metal glinted in the limited light. Frank had a knife and he was going after Lindsay.

Wade crashed through the front door and tripped over Lindsay, landing at Frank Dorian's feet in a heap. Not exactly what he had planned, but at least he was between Frank and Lindsay.

"Well, well. Two for the price of one." Frank chuckled, hooked his arm around Wade's neck and planted the sharp blade against the vein pulsing at the base of Wade's throat.

"Don't know what you see in that bitch. I should have run her off the road that day."

Lindsay gasped. "That was you? You almost killed me and my girls."

"Yeah. I wouldn't be here doing the job now if I had." He tightened his hold on Wade.

"Bastard." Lindsay lurched forward.

"I wouldn't do anything stupid if you want your boyfriend to live."

"Let me guess, Frank, you also set that fire, didn't you?" Wade eased his feet beneath him, the knife pressing into his skin, warm blood oozing down his neck.

"Should have burned this entire place down." Frank jerked his arm up, bringing Wade up higher so that he could get both feet beneath him. "Now things are going to get messy."

"Got that right," Wade said. "I have you right where I want you."

Frank snorted.

Before he could sink the knife into Wade's throat, Wade twisted his body and brought the big man down. In seconds, he had Frank trapped face down beneath him, the man's knife hand pulled up behind his back between his shoulder blades.

"Drop the knife, Frank," Wade demanded.

Frank held tight to the weapon, refusing Wade's order. "You've been a pain in my ass since the day you signed on here, Coltrane."

"Drop it or I break the arm." Wade ratcheted the arm up higher.

Frank grunted and the knife fell from his fingers.

Lindsay scrambled to her feet and grabbed a heavy candle- holder. "Want me to hit him?"

Wade laughed. "Only if it will make you feel better. I have him. Call the police."

"Are you sure?"

"Positive. He's not going anywhere." Wade held tightly to the arm pressed up the middle of Frank's back and pressed his elbow into the man's neck.

Lindsay held the candleholder a few seconds longer, the crazed look in her eyes slowly fading. "Oh God, the girls!"

"They are fine, Lindsay." Wade's words stopped her headlong dash toward the back door. "I gave them orders to hide. They won't come out until we go get them. Will you make that call?"

"Yes, yes. Of course." She reached for the phone on the table beside Henry Kemp's easy chair and held it to her ear. "It's dead."

"He cut the lines." Anger surged anew and Wade pushed Frank's arm higher.

The man grunted. "What did you expect?"

"You like intimidating women, don't you?" Wade asked. "You'll know what intimidation is when you're in jail. Just like your brother."

Frank bucked beneath him. "Leave my brother out of this. He didn't have a chance."

"No, he had his chance. The girl he killed didn't. He got what he deserved and I hope you get the same."

"Bite me, Coltrane."

"Stacy has a cell phone." Lindsay said, her eyes wide. "Stacy!" She ran for the girls' bedroom.

When she returned, she had Stacy with her.

The other woman had a bruise the size of a baseball on her right cheek, but she came out on her own two feet. "My purse is beside the couch. The cell phone is inside."

As Lindsay dived for the phone, Stacy leaned down beside Frank. "I'd kick you in the teeth, but I refuse to sink to your low level, Dorian."

"I should have killed you."

She laughed. "Missed your chance, loser."

"Get me something to tie him up with, will you?" Wade's arm was getting tired of holding the man and he didn't want to give the jerk a chance to escape.

"Got just the thing." Stacy disappeared into the girls' room and reappeared carrying a roll of duct tape. She tore off a piece and slapped it over Frank's mouth. She tore off a longer piece and wrapped it tightly around Dorian's wrist.

Wade brought the other arm behind Frank and Stacy taped his wrists together. Then she went for the feet while Wade sat on his legs.

Lindsay placed the call to the 9-1-1 dispatcher, informing her of what had happened. Lindsay listened for a moment and hung up. "The sheriff will be here—" lights flashed through the windows and Lindsay smiled "—right about now."

"That was fast," Stacy said.

"They were bringing your grandfather home." Wade stood and brushed off his hands.

Sheriff Bernard Hale burst through the door, gun drawn and a deputy behind him, wielding a flashlight. "Everything all right in here?"

Henry Kemp pushed through behind him. "Lindsay?"

"I'm fine, Gramps. Everything is fine."

"The girls?"

"They're hiding. I'll go get them." Wade turned toward the rear of the house, eager to get to his girls and see that they were all right.

"I'll go with you," Lindsay said.

Wade's heart skipped several beats before it resumed, pounding blood through his veins. This would be it. This would be the time she told him she didn't want him around his children, the time she would tell him that the lies between them were too much to overcome.

Wade swallowed hard and nodded. "I understand."

She looked at him her brows dipping briefly, then stepped in front of him, leading the way out the back door.

Lindsay couldn't wait to get to Lyric and Lacey to check them over for any injuries. She could have gone by herself, but sharing the responsibility with Wade of bringing the girls back to the house opened up the opportunity to be alone with him and get a few things straight. "Where are they?"

"I told them to hide in the hayloft and not to come out until you or I came to get them."

"Thanks." She headed for the barn at a swift pace. The girls had to be terrified and crying.

"You were amazing, Lindsay." Wade kept pace with her.

"Thanks for coming to my rescue," she said quietly. "I was running out of options."

"You kept the girls alive when I almost got them killed." Wade's feet slowed. "If I hadn't had your grandfather arrested, you and the girls wouldn't have been alone. I'm sorry."

Lindsay's heart squeezed tightly in her chest. They'd had so many strikes against them from the time Wade left Freedom until now. Could they bridge the gap? Could she forgive him? Could he forgive her?

Stacy's words came to mind. Would she rather

have him any way she could or live the rest of her life without him?

Several feet from the barn door, Lindsay stopped and turned to face Wade, unsure of what she would say, but certain she had to say something.

"You did what you thought you had to do. I can see that now."

Light from the blanket of stars and a full moon shone down on his handsome face, reflecting off the bright blue of his eyes so like her daughters'.

Lindsay continued before she lost her nerve, "I'm sorry I didn't tell you about the girls. I know nothing can make up for the time you lost with them. I should have told you as soon as I knew I was pregnant. I did what I thought I had to do at the time." She realized she was babbling, but she couldn't help it.

Wade reached for her hand and brought it to his cheek. "Lindsay Kemp, I've loved you from the first time I saw you in fifth grade. For years, I wanted you so badly it hurt to be close to you." He inhaled and let it out. "I'm sorry I turned your grandfather in when it was Frank all along. I hope that someday you and Henry will forgive me."

Lindsay's palm cupped his face and a single tear tipped out the corner of her eye and slid down her face. She didn't bother to wipe it away, unable to look away from the love shining at her from Wade's eyes. "I can forgive you." She laughed shakily. "I'm not sure whether Gramps will. Can you ever find it in your heart to forgive me for not telling you about the girls? I'll understand if you don't. I want you to be a part of their lives, no matter what. You will make a terrific father. And maybe someday would you consider marrying me?"

Lindsay clamped a hand to her lips. "Did I just ask you to marry me?" she whispered from behind her fingers.

Wade laughed and pulled her into his arms. "Damn it, woman, if you want this marriage to work out, you will have to let me wear the pants on occasion." Then he kissed her, hard on the lips, his arms so strong around her, telling her more than words could ever express.

"I love you, Wade Coltrane," she said. "I always have."

"I love you, Lindsay. I'd be proud to be your husband. Yes, I will marry you."

"I know you want to be a part of Lyric and Lacey's lives, but you aren't just marrying me for the sake of the girls, are you?" Lindsay asked. "Don't get me wrong, I'll take you any way I can."

"You've had me since the fifth grade. You just didn't know it." He pushed the hair out of her face and brushed the tear from her cheek. "Let's get our daughters before they completely freak out." He slipped his arm around her waist and pulled the barn door open.

"Lacey, Lyric, you can come out now." Wade

switched the light on as he entered the barn. "It's me…Mr. Wade, and your mommy is here."

"I'm here, babies. Come on down." Lindsay stared up at the ladder leading to the loft above.

For a long moment, nothing stirred, then a dark head popped over the railing and gazed down at them, another joining it.

"Mommy! Mr. Wade!" Lacey and Lyric backed up to the ladder and hurried down. As soon as they came within reach, Wade plucked them from the rungs and handed them over to their mother.

They clung to her neck, crying and shaking. Wade wrapped his arms around them all. "It's going to be okay, girls. Mommy is okay, you're okay. The sheriff is taking the bad man away and he'll never come back."

"Want to go back to the house?" Lindsay asked.

Both girls nodded.

"I can't carry you both, though. I wish I could." Lindsay looked to Wade for help.

Wade, his heart swelling, held out his arms. Both Lacey and Lyric reached for him. "Not a problem. I can carry you both." He lifted them from Lindsay's arms and hugged them tightly to his chest.

Hay clung to their pajamas and their hair, their faces were streaked with dirt and tears, but they were the most beautiful little girls a daddy could hope to call his. His eyes stung and he had to blink several times before he could see well enough to walk. When he turned toward the door, Lindsay laid her hand on his arm.

She looked up at him in the light from the bulb hanging overhead. "Tell them."

"I think you should."

"I should have done it a long time ago." Lindsay pushed the hair out of her daughters' faces. "Girls, remember when you asked me if you had a daddy?"

Both girls nodded, sniffling.

"Well, you do." Lindsay smiled, tears welling in her eyes. "Mr. Wade is your daddy."

The girls looked at him as if staring at a stranger, their eyes narrowing. "Where were you?" Lyric asked.

Wade's chest hurt like someone was squeezing it in a giant fist. "I was a soldier fighting in a war." A war that hadn't ended in his heart until that very moment. His gut tightened, butterflies flitting around as they continued to frown.

"You're our daddy?" Lacey asked, her hands reaching out to touch his face, his ears, his beard. "I didn't know a daddy was fuzzy."

Wade grinned. "I can shave it."

Lyric wrapped her arms around his neck and pressed her cheek to his beard. "I like it. It tickles my face." She giggled.

Lacey tried it and giggled, too. "Daddy, can you teach me to ride Thunder?"

"Thunder?" Wade's eyes widened, the knot in his

belly loosening, happiness filling him to full and overflowing. His daughter had called him daddy.

Lindsay patted her daughters' backs. "We need to get back to the house. Gramps will be worried about you and it's way past bedtime."

"Do we have to go to bed?" Lyric asked, hooking her arm around Wade's neck. "I want to stay up and play with my daddy."

"I'll be here tomorrow, darlin'." He kissed her cheek and hugged her tight.

"Will you sleep in our room?" Lacey's arms slipped around his neck and she buried her head in the curve of his neck. "I'm scared."

"Yes, I'll sleep in your room if you want."

As they entered the house, the girls clung to Wade, their bodies quivering. The sheriff had taken Frank away in his SUV.

Wade had to carry the girls through the house, peering under beds and into closets to prove to them the bad man was truly gone.

As promised, Wade arranged a pallet on the floor between their twin beds and he lay down with them until they finally fell asleep.

After her shower, Lindsay crept in and lay down beside Wade.

"This is nice," she said, snuggling against him.

"They wanted me to read them a story about a princess."

"Get used to it." Lindsay chuckled. "They want

that same story every night. I think I can recite it with my eyes closed."

Wade stared up at the glow of the nightlight reflecting off the ceiling. He had unfinished business that needed resolving and he wasn't sure how to start.

Lindsay leaned up on her elbow and stared down at him. "What's wrong? Second thoughts?" She ran a finger along his cheek, finding and tracing the line of the scar he'd gotten while in captivity.

"No second thoughts on my part, but you might want to reconsider." Wade captured her finger and kissed the tip. "There are things you need to know about me, about my stint in the military."

"I'm listening."

How did he tell her what had happened? More afraid than he'd been facing torture from a terrorist, Wade took a breath and jumped in. He didn't have any idea how long he talked, but all the story came out in a quiet rush as if he'd opened the dam and couldn't stop the flow once it started.

When he came to the end where he'd lost faith in himself and quit the military, his words trickled to a stop and he waited for Lindsay to say something. Praying she didn't pity him. He couldn't stand it if she pitied him.

"Wow, I never knew what you were going through. I couldn't have lasted as long as you did."

"By giving up that information, I betrayed my

unit, my country and myself. Can you live with less than a man?"

"Wade." Lindsay kissed the scar on his face. "To me you're more than a man. You're a hero."

He shook his head, opening his mouth to protest her words.

Lindsay placed a finger over her lips and continued quietly, "You were tortured. You held out as long as humanly possible. You have to forgive yourself or you'll never get over it."

Wade captured her finger and opened her palm to kiss the calluses she'd grown from all the work she did with the kids and horses. "You deserve better, Lindsay Kemp."

"You're not backing out on me now. I asked, you said yes. It's a contract, legal and binding." She captured his face in her hands and kissed him. "It doesn't change anything. I still love you. You're still a good man. You did what you had to do to survive. Now I need you to love me and the two little girls who are beyond excited to know that they have a daddy."

"That will be the easiest assignment I've ever taken." Wade wrapped Lindsay in his arms and kissed her soundly. He might not get over his guilt at caving under duress, but having Lindsay and the girls would go a long way toward creating new memories so that the old ones could eventually fade.

"What about your grandfather? Think he'll

get out the shotgun and chase me off the Long K Ranch?"

"Not a chance."

"When will we tell him?"

"Likely he's got a clue something's afoot. But let's wait until after dinner tomorrow. We have to go to the courthouse in the morning and give sworn statements about what happened here tonight." Lindsay sighed. "Gramps always knew the girls were yours, but he never let on. Sometimes I don't get that man."

THE NEXT DAY was a flurry of activities. Between a trip to the sheriff's office to give their statements and lunch with the girls at the Talk of the Town, Lindsay and Wade hadn't had time to slow down.

Lindsay's grandfather had been mysteriously absent for most of that time and she wondered what he was up to.

Wade surprised her with one final stop at the local jewelry store to select an engagement ring. The girls helped and they came out with a ring they all loved.

Lindsay cooked the evening meal as usual, but her grandfather had called to say he'd be in town for dinner.

After the dishes had been cleared away, Lindsay and Wade sat in the living room with mugs of coffee, waiting for Henry Kemp.

"Good grief, where has that man gotten to?"

Lindsay looked at the clock for the tenth time in as many minutes. "It's not like him to stay out past dark."

The girls were dressed for bed and playing with dolls in the room. Before long it would be time for Lindsay to read them a story and tuck them in. Where was her grandfather?

Lindsay's grandfather knew Wade was the father of her children. Would he still be angry that Wade had snooped through his desk drawers and then called the sheriff to have him arrested? Would he kick Wade off the ranch? If he did, there was no question that Lindsay and the girls would go with him. The girls would have to get used to the idea of living somewhere else besides the Long K Ranch.

So much rode on Henry Kemp's response and attitude toward his future grandson-in-law.

Headlights shone through the window and soon boots clumped across the porch. Henry Kemp strode through the front door and into the living room. Without a word, he sat in his easy chair and stared across the floor at Wade and Lindsay. "What do you two have to say for yourselves?" he demanded.

Lindsay's heart skipped several beats as she scrambled for words.

Wade took her hand in his and looked across the room at her grandfather. "Sir, please accept my apologies for going through your desk and for jumping to conclusions about the knife and nails I found."

Henry Kemp raised his hand. "Had a conversation with Bart Bellows on the telephone while you two were out giving statements. He explained everything."

"Still, I'm sorry I betrayed your trust in me."

"Me, too." The older man's eyes narrowed for a moment, then his bushy white brows rose. "But seeing as my big mouth was flappin' and I was bellyachin' loud enough to anyone who'd listen, guess I brought the suspicion on myself."

Lindsay smiled at her grandfather, relieved he wasn't too upset about being arrested. "Gramps, you've just gotta let it go about the land you sold the Lockharts."

For the first time since Wade could remember, Henry Kemp nodded in agreement. "You're absolutely right. Besides, I can't bellyache when I got a rich oilfield right underneath the pasture that burned the other day." Henry Kemp slapped his knee and laughed out loud. "Lindsay, girl, our troubles are soon to be over."

Lindsay tipped her head, her forehead wrinkling. "What are you talking about, Gramps?"

"I wasn't gonna tell you until I was sure. Now I am—sure, that is. I had one of those oil speculators snooping around the ranch. He had a geologist come out and perform some newfangled tests and they are so certain there's oil on this land that they were willing to pay me up front for the right to drill on my property."

Lindsay leaned forward. "Are you positive they weren't shysters?"

"Yup. I had my lawyer look them up. They run a legitimate business and they transferred the money to our bank account today."

Lindsay sucked in a breath and let it out slowly. "How much, Gramps?"

"Enough we can pay the ranch hands for the rest of the year. Enough to pay the mortgage for the next four years. You can quit teaching riding lessons if you want."

"I like teaching." Lindsay leaned back in her chair, a grin spreading across her face. "We get to keep the ranch. Oh, thank God, we get to keep the ranch."

"Yup and if the oil is there, like they think it is, we won't have to worry about a thing from now on."

Lindsay hugged Wade's arm. "That's great news. The girls thought we were going to have to move." Lindsay sat up again and she looked at Wade. "That is…well…" she mumbled to a stop.

"What Lindsay is trying to say is, if it's all right with you, we'd like to get married. Where we live hasn't yet been decided."

Henry slapped his hand on the arm of his chair and bellowed, "'Bout damn time. Thought you'd never get around to asking that poor girl."

Wade slipped his arm around Lindsay. "I've

wanted to since we were kids in high school. I was just too stupid to get it out, apparently."

"You two are living here," Gramps stated. "That's if you can put up with a grumpy old man."

Lindsay looked to Wade. "I'll go wherever you want me to go, but the girls love it here."

"As long as I can do my part. I won't live off you two. I have a job working for Bart Bellows's Corps Security and Investigations team. Living here would be a good idea as I'll be on the road for some of my assignments. When I'm here, I can do my part and help with the ranch."

"Good, good. It's settled, then. Glad to have you on board with my Lindsay." He picked up the remote for the television and hit the on button. The evening news report flashed on the screen with Lila Lockhart standing in front of the capitol in Austin, an information flag in the left-hand corner of the screen indicating the newscast was live.

"Can't get away from those damn Lockharts, can I?" Gramps lifted the remote, ready to punch in a new channel selection.

"Wait, Gramps." Lindsay held up her hand. "Let's see what she has to say."

"I didn't know she was in Austin." Wade leaned back so that Lindsay could see around him. "She must have driven out there last night or this morning."

"Look, ain't that Bart Bellows beside her?" Henry leaned forward again.

"Shh." Lindsay held a finger to her lips. "She's saying something."

A reporter shouted out, "Governor Lockhart, what happened at the fundraiser in Freedom yesterday?"

Lila Lockhart looked directly into the camera and smiled. "We had what we call in Freedom a little incident. But now that the threat to myself and my family has been neutralized, I'm pleased to announce that I will be throwing my hat into the ring for the presidential election."

"Well, I'll be damned." Henry Kemp sat back in his chair. "That woman's got more gumption than a blind mouse in a pit full of rattlesnakes."

"Thank goodness we caught Frank. Let's hope Governor Lockhart doesn't have any other troubles." Lindsay grinned and squeezed Wade's hand. "How refreshing, a woman running for president."

The crowd roared as Lila Lockhart, followed by Bart Bellows, left the podium and moved toward the ramp leading down to street level, shaking hands with well-wishers as she went.

Just as Lila stepped onto the ramp, the stage erupted, tossing the podium into the sea of reporters. The camera shook and someone cursed before the screen went black.

"What the heck?" Henry yelled.

The girls ran into the room, wide-eyed.

Lyric pushed her way between Lindsay and Wade's knees. "What's wrong?"

Wade's phone vibrated in his pocket, tickling Lindsay's hip.

He leaned back, pulled the phone out and flipped it open. "Coltrane." Everyone sat in silence, even the girls, as Wade listened to a voice talking fast and furious on the other end.

Lindsay held her breath, feeling the tension building in Wade as the silence in the room stretched on.

"Yes, sir. I will." Wade flipped the phone shut, rose from his seat and planted his Stetson on his head. "I have to go. All Corps Security and Investigations agents have been placed on alert." He bent to kiss the tops of the girls' heads. "Take care of your mommy while I'm away."

Lindsay stood and walked him to the door. "Do me a favor, will ya?" She leaned up on her toes to brush a kiss across his lips. "Don't be gone for five years this time."

"Wild horses couldn't keep me away." He gathered her into his arms and kissed her soundly. "Don't wait up for me. But don't worry, I *will* be home."

* * * * *

LARGER-PRINT BOOKS!

GET 2 FREE LARGER-PRINT NOVELS PLUS
2 FREE GIFTS!

⌐ Harlequin®

INTRIGUE®

BREATHTAKING ROMANTIC SUSPENSE

YES! Please send me 2 FREE LARGER-PRINT Harlequin Intrigue® novels and my 2 FREE gifts (gifts are worth about $10). After receiving them, if I don't wish to receive any more books, I can return the shipping statement marked "cancel." If I don't cancel, I will receive 6 brand-new novels every month and be billed just $4.99 per book in the U.S. or $5.74 per book in Canada. That's a saving of at least 13% off the cover price! It's quite a bargain! Shipping and handling is just 50¢ per book in the U.S. and 75¢ per book in Canada.* I understand that accepting the 2 free books and gifts places me under no obligation to buy anything. I can always return a shipment and cancel at any time. Even if I never buy another book, the two free books and gifts are mine to keep forever.

199/399 HDN FC7W

Name _____ (PLEASE PRINT)

Address _____ Apt. #

City _____ State/Prov. _____ Zip/Postal Code

Signature (if under 18, a parent or guardian must sign)

Mail to the **Reader Service:**
IN U.S.A.: P.O. Box 1867, Buffalo, NY 14240-1867
IN CANADA: P.O. Box 609, Fort Erie, Ontario L2A 5X3

Not valid for current subscribers to Harlequin Intrigue Larger-Print books.

**Are you a subscriber to Harlequin Intrigue books
and want to receive the larger-print edition?
Call 1-800-873-8635 today or visit www.ReaderService.com.**

* Terms and prices subject to change without notice. Prices do not include applicable taxes. Sales tax applicable in N.Y. Canadian residents will be charged applicable taxes. Offer not valid in Quebec. This offer is limited to one order per household. All orders subject to credit approval. Credit or debit balances in a customer's account(s) may be offset by any other outstanding balance owed by or to the customer. Please allow 4 to 6 weeks for delivery. Offer available while quantities last.

Your Privacy—The Reader Service is committed to protecting your privacy. Our Privacy Policy is available online at www.ReaderService.com or upon request from the Reader Service.

We make a portion of our mailing list available to reputable third parties that offer products we believe may interest you. If you prefer that we not exchange your name with third parties, or if you wish to clarify or modify your communication preferences, please visit us at www.ReaderService.com/consumerschoice or write to us at Reader Service Preference Service, P.O. Box 9062, Buffalo, NY 14269. Include your complete name and address.

HILP11